A BURNING

A BURNING

Megha Majumdar

Alfred A. Knopf

New York · 2020

THIS IS A BORZOI BOOK
PUBLISHED BY ALFRED A. KNOPF

www.aaknopf.com

Knopf, Borzoi Books, and the colophon are registered
trademarks of Penguin Random House LLC.

Library of Congress Cataloging-in-Publication Data
Names: Majumdar, Megha, author.
Title: A burning / Megha Majumdar.
Description: First edition. | New York :
Alfred A. Knopf, 2020.
Identifiers: LCCN 2019039498 (print) |
LCCN 2019039499 (ebook) |
ISBN 9780525658696 (hardcover) |
ISBN 9780525658702 (ebook) |
ISBN 9781524711788 (open market)
Subjects: GSAFD: Suspense fiction.
Classification: LCC PS3613.A35388 B87 2020 (print) |
LCC PS3613.A35388 (ebook) | DDC 813/.6—dc23
LC record available at
https://lccn.loc.gov/2019039498
LC ebook record available at
https://lccn.loc.gov/2019039499

Jacket design by Tyler Comrie

Manufactured in the United States of America
Published June 2, 2020
Second Printing, June 2020

For my mother and father,
who have made everything possible

A BURNING

JIVAN

"YOU SMELL LIKE SMOKE," MY MOTHER SAID TO ME.

So I rubbed an oval of soap in my hair and poured a whole bucket of water on myself before a neighbor complained that I was wasting the morning supply.

There was a curfew that day. On the main street, a police jeep would creep by every half hour. Daily-wage laborers, compelled to work, would come home with arms raised to show they had no weapons.

In bed, my wet hair spread on the pillow, I picked up my new phone—purchased with my own salary, screen guard still attached.

On Facebook, there was only one conversation.

These terrorists attacked the wrong neighborhood #KolabaganTrainAttack #Undefeated

Friends, if you have fifty rupees, skip your samosas today and donate to—

The more I scrolled, the more Facebook unrolled.

This news clip exclusively from 24 Hours shows how—

Candlelight vigil at—

The night before, I had been at the railway station, no more than a fifteen-minute walk from my house. I ought to have seen the men who stole up to the open windows and threw flaming torches into the halted train. But all I saw were carriages, burning, their doors locked from the outside and dangerously hot. The fire spread to huts bordering the station, smoke filling the chests of those who lived there. More than a hundred people died. The government promised compensation to the families of the dead—eighty thousand rupees!—which, well, the government promises many things.

In a video, to the dozen microphones thrust at his chin, the chief minister was saying, "Let the authorities investigate." Somebody had spliced this comment with a video of policemen scratching their heads. It made me laugh.

I admired these strangers on Facebook who said anything they wanted to. They were not afraid of making jokes. Whether it was about the police or the ministers, they had their fun, and wasn't that freedom? I hoped that after a few more salary slips, after I rose to be a senior sales clerk of Pantaloons, I would be free in that way too.

Then, in a video clip further down the page, a woman came forward, her hair flying, her nose running a wet trail down to her lips, her eyes red. She was standing on the sloping platform of our small railway station. Into the microphone she screamed: "There was a jeep full of policemen right there. Ask them why they stood around and watched while my husband burned. He tried to open the door and save my daughter. He tried and tried."

I shared that video. I added a caption.

Policemen paid by the government watched and did nothing while this innocent woman lost everything, I wrote.

I laid the phone next to my head, and dozed. The heat brought sleep to my eyes. When I checked my phone next, there were only two likes. A half hour later, still two likes.

Then a woman, I don't know who, commented on my post, *How do you know this person is not faking it? Maybe she wants attention!*

I sat up. Was I friends with this person? In her profile picture she was posing in a bathroom.

Did you even watch the video? I replied.

The words of the heartless woman drifted in my mind. I was irritated by her, but there was excitement too. This was not the frustration of no water in the municipal pump or power cut on the hottest night. Wasn't this a kind of leisure dressed up as agitation?

For me, the day was a holiday, after all. My mother was cooking fish so small we would eat them bones and tail. My father was taking in the sun, his back pain eased.

Under my thumb, I watched post after post about the train attack earn fifty likes, a hundred likes, three hundred likes. Nobody liked my reply.

And then, in the small, glowing screen, I wrote a foolish thing. I wrote a dangerous thing, a thing nobody like me should ever think, let alone write.

Forgive me, Ma.

If the police didn't help ordinary people like you and

me, if the police watched them die, doesn't that mean, I wrote on Facebook, *that the government is also a terrorist?*

Outside the door, a man slowly pedaled his rickshaw, the only passenger his child, the horn going *paw paw* for her glee.

LOVELY

SUNDAY MORNING! TIME TO GO TO ACTING CLASS.
With my hips swinging like this and like that, I am
walking past the guava seller.

"Brother," I am calling, "what's the time?"

"Eight thirty," he is grumbling, because he is not
wishing to share with me the fruits of his wristwatch.
Leave him. I am abandoning my stylish walk and
running like a horse to the local railway station. On
the train, while I am touching my chest and forehead,
saying a prayer for those poor people who were dying
a few days ago at this very station—

"Who is pushing?" one aunty is shouting. "Stop it!"

"This hijra couldn't find a different compartment
to hassle?" the peanut seller is hissing, as if I am not
having ears.

Nothing is simple for a person like me, not even
one hour on the train. My chest is a man's chest,
and my breasts are made of rags. So what? Find me
another woman in this whole city as truly woman
as me.

In the middle of this crowd a legless beggar is

coming down the corridor, sitting on a wheeled plank of wood which he is rolling on everybody's feet.

"Give me one coin," he is whining.

People are yelling at him.

"Now you need to pass?"

"No eyes or what?"

"Where will I stand, on your head?"

Now he is also shouting back, "Let me cut off your legs, then you see how you manage!"

It is true to god making me laugh and laugh. This is why I am liking the local trains. You can be burning one train, but you cannot be stopping our will to go to work, to class, to family if we have them. Every local train is like a film. On the train, I am observing faces, body movements, voices, fights. This is how people like me are learning. When this train is swaying, picking up speed, wind whipping my hair, I am putting my fingertips on the ceiling, making my body straight and tall for Mr. Debnath's acting class.

*

AT MR. DEBNATH'S HOUSE, he is resting in a chair, drinking tea from a saucer. That way the tea is cooling fast and he is not having to do *phoo phoo*.

I have heard of acting coaches who are taking advantage of strugglers. But Mr. Debnath is not like that. He is having morals. In his younger days he was getting a chance to direct a film himself, but the opportunity was in Bombay. So he was having to go to Bombay for six months, minimum. At that time his old mother was in a hospital. What kind of monster would abandon his mother to chase his dreams? So he was sacrificing his own goals and staying with his mother. When he was telling us this sad story, it was the only time I was seeing him cry.

Next to his feet are sitting six other students. Brijesh, who is working as an electrician; Rumeli, who is selling magic ointment for rashes; Peonji, who is working as a clerk in the insurance office; Radha, who is studying how to be a nurse; and Joyita, who is doing bookkeeping in her father's pen refill business. Nobody is really sure what Kumar is doing because he is only laughing in answer to all questions.

We are all saving and saving, and handing over fifty rupees each class.

Today, in this living room which is our stage, we are pushing the dining table to one side, and practicing a scene in which a man is being suspicious of his wife. After some, if it can be said, lackluster performances, it is my turn. I am placing my phone on the floor to record myself for study purposes, then going to the center of the room and rolling my neck, left to right, right to left. Mr. Debnath's deceased parents, please to pray for them, are looking at me with strict faces from photos on the wall. I am feeling hot, even though the fan is running on maximum speed.

Time for my artistic performance. This time my partner is Brijesh, the electrician. According to the script that Mr. Debnath is giving us, Brijesh, now the suspicious husband, is having to hold my shoulders forcefully, angrily. But he is holding my shoulders too lightly. I am being forced to leave my character.

"Not like that!" I am saying. "If you are holding me like a petal, how will I have the strong feeling? You have to give it to me, the anger, the frustration! Come on!"

Mr. Debnath is approving of this. If you are not feeling it, he is always saying, how will your audience be feeling it? So I am hitting Brijesh's shoulder a little, making him a bit angry, showing him that he can be a little more manly with me. He is mumbling something, so I am saying, "What? Say it loudly."

After a long time Brijesh is finally saying, "Uff! Don't make me say it, Lovely. I can't do this marriage scene with a half man."

At this time the clock is gonging eleven times, making us all silent. My cheeks are getting hot. Oh I am used to this—on the road, on the train, at the shops. But in my acting class? With Brijesh?

So I am just throwing away his insult. It is garbage.

"Listen, Brijesh," I am saying, "you are like my brother. So if I can act romantic with you, then you can also act romantic with me!"

"That's right," Mr. Debnath is saying. "If you are serious about films, you have to be fully in your role—"

He is giving Brijesh a real lecture. When he is pausing, you can even hear the ticking of the big clock on the wall.

Finally Brijesh is joining his hands to beg forgiveness from me, per Mr. Debnath's suggestion, and I am having a few tears in my eyes also. Rumeli is blowing her nose into her dupatta. Mr. Debnath is clapping his hands and saying, "Channel this emotion into your scene!"

The moment is full of tension. The other students are putting their mobile phones away when I am roaring: "You have the audacity to hit a mother!"

This character's rage, I am feeling it in my chest. This living room, with chair and table pushed to the corner, with cabinet full of dusty teddies, is nothing less than a stage in Bombay. The tubelight is as bright as a spotlight shining on me. Outside, a pillow filler is walking by, twanging his cotton-sorting instrument like a harp. Only windows, with thin curtains, are separating me from the nobodies on the street.

Then, holding the emotion but lowering my voice, I am delivering the next line: "Have you not fallen from your mother's womb?"

Brijesh: "Mother, hah, as if you have that dignity! You think I don't know about *him*?"

Me: "I swear it's not what you are thinking. Let me explain. Oh, please give me one chance to explain."

Brijesh: (stone-faced, looking out of imaginary window)

Me: "I was never wanting to talk about my past, but you are forcing me. So now I have to tell you my secret. It is not me who has been with that man. It is my twin sister."

What dialogue! The scene ends.

My palms are chilled and sweating. But my heart is light like a kite. There is thundering silence in the room. Even the maid is watching from the doorway, both broom and dustpan in her hand. Her jaw is falling open. Seeing her, I am feeling like smiling. I am finally coming out of the scene and back into the room.

Mr. Debnath is looking a bit crazed.

"This is how you do it!" he is whispering. His eyes are big. He is trying to put on his sandals and stand up from the chair, but one sandal is sliding away every time he is putting his foot on it. Never mind, he is looking very serious.

"My students, see how she used her voice?" he is saying. "See how she was feeling it, and that feeling was being transferred to you?" Spit is flying from his mouth, showering the heads of his students.

Radha, who is sitting below him, is tearing a corner of the newspaper on the floor. Then she is wiping her hair with it.

Almost one year ago I was coming to Mr. Debnath's house for the first time. He was asking to take my interview in the street. Because—he was saying, this was his explanation—the house was being painted, so there was nowhere to sit.

Rubbish. Where were the painters, the rags, the buckets, the ladders?

I was knowing the truth. The truth was that Mrs. Debnath was not wanting a hijra in the house.

So I was standing in the street, making sure a passing rickshaw was not hitting my behind. Mr. Debnath was saying, "Why you are so bent on acting? It's too hard!"

My kohl was smearing and my lipstick was gone on some cup of tea. My armpits were stinking, my black hair was absorbing all the heat of the day and giving me a headache. But this was the one question I was always able to answer.

"I have been performing all my life," I was saying to him. I was performing on trains, on roads. I was performing happiness and cheer. I was performing divine connection. "Now," I was telling him, "just let me practice for the camera."

Today, I am standing up and joining my hands. I am bowing. What else to do when there is so much clapping? They are clapping and clapping, my fans. My bookkeeper fan, my ointment-seller fan, my insurance-clerk fan. Even when I am waving my hand, smiling too broadly, saying, "Stop it!" they are going on clapping.

JIVAN

A FEW NIGHTS LATER, THERE WAS A KNOCKING. IT was late, two or three a.m., when any sound brings your heart to your throat. My mother was shouting, "Wake up, wake up!"

A hand reached out of the dark and dragged me up in my nightie. I screamed and fought, believing it was a man come to do what men do. But it was a policewoman.

My father, on the floor, his throat dry and his painful back rigid, mewled. Nighttime turned him into a child.

Then I was in the back of the police van, watching through the wire mesh a view of roads glowing orange under streetlamps. I exhausted myself appealing to the policewoman and group of policemen sitting in front of me: "Sister, what is happening? I am a working girl. I work at Pantaloons. I have nothing to do with police!"

They said nothing. Now and then a crackle came from the radio on the dashboard, far in front. At some point, a car filled with boys sped by, and I heard whooping and cheering. They were coming from a nightclub. The doddering police van meant nothing to those boys. They did not slow down. They were not afraid. Their fathers knew police commissioners and members of the legislature, figures who were capable of making all problems disappear. And me, how would I get out of this? Whom did I know?

LOVELY

AT NIGHT, AFTER THE ACTING CLASS, I AM LYING IN
bed with Azad, my husband, my businessman who
is buying and reselling *Sansung* electronics and *Tony
Hilfiger* wristwatches from Chinese ships docking
in Diamond Harbor. I am showing him my practice
video from the day's class, and now he is saying, "I
have been telling you for hundred years! You have
star material in you!"

He is pinching my cheek, and I am laughing even
though it is hurting. I am feeling peaceful, like this
thin mattress on the floor is our own luxury five-star
hotel bed. In this room I am having everything I am
needing. A jar of drinking water, some dishes, a small
kerosene stove, and a shelf for my clothes and jew-
elry. On the wall, giving me their blessings every day,
are Priyanka Chopra and Shah Rukh Khan. When I
am looking around, I am seeing their beautiful faces,
and some of their good fortune is sprinkling down
on me.

*

"AZAD," I AM SAYING this night. My face is close to his face, like we are in a romantic scene in a blockbuster. "Promise you will not get angry if I am telling you something?"

I am taking a moment to look at his face, dark and gray. Some long hairs in his eyebrows trying to escape. I am having difficulty looking eye to eye for these hard words.

"Aren't you thinking," I am saying finally, "about family and all? We are not so young—"

Azad is starting to talk over me, like always. "Again?" he is saying. I am knowing that he is annoyed. "Was my brother coming here?"

"No!"

"Was my brother putting this rubbish in your head?"

"No, I am telling you!"

Why Azad is always accusing me of such things?

"Everyone knows it is the way of the world, Azad," I am telling him. "Yes, the world is backward, and yes, the world is stupid. But your family is wanting you to marry a proper woman, have children. And look at me—I can never give you a future like that."

Immediately, I am regretting. This is a great big mistake. I am wishing to be with Azad always, so why I am pushing him away?

*

ACTUALLY, AZAD IS RIGHT. His brother was coming one night. He was coming before dawn, ringing the bell, banging his fist on the door. He was making such a racket the street dogs were barking *gheu gheu*.

When I was finally leaping out of bed and unlatching the door, Azad's brother was immediately shouting at my face, "Whatever curse you have given him, let him go, witch!"

"Shhh!" I was saying. "Be quiet, it's the middle of the night!"

"Don't you tell me what to do, witch!" he was screaming, wagging a finger in the air. One man pissing in the gutter was looking at him, then at me, then at him, then at me. Otherwise, all was quiet and dark, but surely everybody was hearing everything.

"You have trapped him!" this brother was screaming. "Now you have to free him! Let him get married like a normal person!"

I was only standing, holding the open door. "Calm yourself," I was saying quietly. "You will make yourself sick."

I was wearing my nightie. My ears were burning. The whole neighborhood was learning my business. Now this was making me angry. Who was giving this good-for-nothing brother the right to shout at me in front of the whole locality? All these people were hardworking rickshaw pullers, fruit sellers, cotton fillers, maidservants, guards in the malls. They were needing sleep. Now what respect was I having left in their eyes?

So finally I was shouting back some rude things. I don't like remembering them.

*

"OKAY," I AM ADMITTING to Azad now. "Fine, your brother came. He was saying to me, 'Lovely, I know your love is true. My brother refuses to even eat if you are not there. But please, I am begging, talk to him about marriage and children, for our old parents' sake.'"

Azad is looking at me. "My brother? Said that?"

He is not believing his ears.

"Yes, your own brother," I am saying. "So I am thinking about it."

A spider with thin brown legs is crawling through the window. With all eight legs it is exploring the wall. Both of us are watching it. When Azad is getting up and about to slap the spider with his shoe, I am saying, "Leave it."

Why to always ruin other creatures' lives?

"No!" Azad is saying. "I am not going to follow such stupid rules! I will marry *you*!"

JIVAN

THE NEXT MORNING, AT THE COURTHOUSE, A POLICE-
woman opens for me a path through a crowd moving like they are joyous, like they are celebrating at
a cricket stadium. The sun blazes in my eyes. I look
at the ground.

"Jivan! Jivan! Look here," shout reporters with
cameras mounted on their shoulders or raised high
above their heads. Some reporters reach forward to
push recorders toward my mouth, though policemen
beat them back. I am jostled and shoved, my feet
stepped on, my elbows knocked into my ribs. These
men shout questions.

"How did the terrorists make contact with you?"

"When did you start planning the attack?"

I find my voice and shout, a brief cry which dies
down like a rooster's: "I am innocent! I don't know
anything about—"

I stand tall, though colors appear bright in my
eyes, the greens of trees luminous as a mineral seam,
the ground beneath my feet composed of distinct par-

ticles. My legs buckle, and the policewoman catches me. A shout goes up among the crowd. The policewoman's grip on my arm is the kindest thing. Then indoors, where the noise recedes and I am allowed to slump in a chair.

A lawyer appointed to me appears. He is young, only a little older than me, though he has the potbelly of a wealthy man.

"Did you get food this morning?" is the first thing he says.

I look at my policewomen handlers and cannot remember. I nod.

"I am Gobind," he says. "Your court-appointed lawyer. Do you understand what 'lawyer' means? It means that—"

"Sir," I begin. "I understand what it means. I went to school. I am a sales clerk at Pantaloons, you know that shop? You tell me this, why am I arrested? Fine, I posted one stupid thing on Facebook, but I don't know anything about the train."

The lawyer looks not at me but at a folder in his hands. He licks a finger and turns the pages.

"Are you telling the truth?" he says. "They found your chat records talking to the terrorist recruiter on Facebook."

"Everybody keeps saying this to me, but this boy was just someone I chatted with online. We were online friends," I plead. "I didn't know who he was."

From my chair, I hear the wheeze of a ceiling fan above me, and the chatter of visitors entering the courtroom behind. In front, all I see is an aunty sitting at a typewriter. Tendrils of hair slip loose from the coil at the base of her neck.

"On Facebook I made many friends, including this friend in a foreign country. At least, that is what he told me," I explain to Gobind. "This friend asked me about my life, and my feelings. I sent him emojis sometimes, to say hello. Now they tell me he was a known terrorist recruiter. Known to whom? I didn't know any of this."

Gobind looks at me. A woman like me is never believed.

"What about these cloths soaked in kerosene found at your house?" says Gobind after a while. "Very much like the kerosene-soaked torches that were tossed into the train. What about that?"

"Those were . . ." I think hard. "Probably my mother's cleaning cloths. Kerosene to get grease off. I don't know! I have never seen them."

They say I helped terrorists set fire to the train. Not only do they have Facebook chat records with a man I now know is a recruiter, there were witnesses at the railway station who saw me walking to the train station with a package in my arms. Must have been kerosene, they say. Must have been rags, or wood for torches. Other witnesses saw me running away from the train, with no package in my arms. Though they saw no men with me, they allege that I guided men, terrorists, enemies of the country, down the unnamed lanes of my slum, to the station where the cursed train would be waiting.

When I protest my innocence, they point to the seditious statements I posted on Facebook, calling my own government a "terrorist" and showing, so they say, a marked absence of loyalty to the state. Is it a crime to write some words on Facebook?

Gobind points to a document I signed while in police lockup. He tells me I confessed.

"Who believes that?" I charge. "They forced me to sign. They were beating me."

I turn to the courtroom, wishing for my mother and father to be here, for their soothing hand on my head, at the same time as I wish for them to never see me here. They would not be able to bear it.

Then the judge arrives, and reads a list of charges.

"Crimes against the nation," he says. "Sedition."

I hear the words. I raise my hand and gesture no, no, no.

"I was taking a few books, my schoolbooks," I say. It is the truth, so why does it sound so meager? "That was my package. I was taking my schoolbooks to a person in the slum. Her name is Lovely. Ask her. She will tell you that I was teaching her English for some months."

From the back, a voice scoffs, "Keep your stories for the papers. A terrorist doing charity! What an A-plus story! The media will eat it up!"

The judge threatens to throw the voice out of the room.

"They made me sign the confession," I tell the judge later. I lift my tunic to reveal my bruised abdomen, and hear people shift behind me.

This time the judge listens, his eyebrows raised.

Days later, in a newspaper, I will see an artist's drawing of me appearing in court that morning. The sketch shows a woman with her hair in a braid. Her hands are cuffed but raised as in prayer or plea. This is a mistake, I think. I was not in cuffs. Was I? The rest of her body is hastily penciled, decaying already.

JIVAN'S MOTHER
AND FATHER

NO MORE THAN AN HOUR AFTER JIVAN WAS ARRESTED, a reporter found the house in the slum and knocked. The door was a sheet of tin, unlatched. It fell open. Jivan's mother was sitting by Jivan's father on the raised bed, and fanning him with a folded newspaper.

At the sight of the reporter, Jivan's mother rose and walked to the door. "Who are you?" she demanded. "Are you police?"

The newsman held a recorder at a respectful distance and said, "*Daily Beacon*. I am Purnendu Sarkar." He flipped open his wallet to show her ID, then tucked it into a back pocket. "Do you know why your daughter has been arrested?"

Jivan's mother said, "They will send a policeman with the information, that is what they told me. Where did they take Jivan?"

This mother was confused, the reporter saw. She did not know anything. He sighed. Then he turned off his recorder, and told her what he knew.

"Mother," he said in the end, "did you understand what I said?"

"Why would I not understand," said she. "I am her mother!"

And to her husband she turned. Jivan's father, stiff-backed on the bed, knew, had known, something terrible was happening.

"They are saying something about Jivan," she cried. "Come here and see, what are they saying?"

But her husband only lifted his head, sensing a frightening disturbance in the night. He moved his dry mouth to speak, and stopped. His chin trembled, and his arm, raised from the elbow, hailed somebody for help.

A figure peeled away from the carrom players outside. He was Kalu the neighbor, with his bulging neck tumor. By that time, more reporters had arrived, and a curious crowd had formed outside the house. This crowd made way for him in fear and disgust. Kalu shut the door behind him, and a shout of protest went up from the gathered reporters.

"Mother," he said, "have you eaten? Then let's go. These people are saying they know where Jivan is."

Then he took her, sitting on the back of his motorcycle, her legs dangling like a schoolgirl's, to the police station the reporters had named. By the time Jivan's mother stepped off the motorcycle, in her arms nothing but an envelope, much crushed—her daughter's birth certificate, school-leaving certificate, polio drop receipt, for documents were all she had—the sky was turning from black to blue.

Jivan's mother made her way to the entrance of the police station, where, she had been told, her daughter was held. There was a crowd of reporters here too. They had lights and cameras. One reporter applied lipstick, while another crushed a cigarette underfoot. At the gate stood two guards, rifles strapped to their backs. Periodically they shouted at the journalists to step back. Otherwise they leaned in the doorway, chatting.

They turned to look at the stooped woman who came right up to them, her feet in bathroom slippers.

"Stop, stop," one said. "Where are you going? Can't you see this is a police station?"

Jivan's mother told them she was there to see her child.

"Who is your son?" said the guard, irritated, while his friend wandered away.

"My daughter. Jivan, she is called."

The guard's mouth fell open. Here she was, the mother of the terrorist.

"Not now," he said finally. "No visiting in the lockup."

The guard, on order to let nobody meet with the terrorist, refused to let her mother in.

JIVAN

EARLY ONE MORNING, A MAN APPEARS OUTSIDE MY cell, holding in his hands a foolscap sheet of paper. "Undertrials!" he barks.

A line of filthy men forms. The men wear slippers rubbed thin at the heels, and vests pasted to their sweating chests. One shouts, "Is this the line for omelets?"

A few of the men laugh, no mirth in their voices.

Some say nothing, watching the specimen of me in my cell. I am to stay in prison until my trial a year later.

The man in charge unlocks the gate and pokes his head in.

"You, madam! You need a special invitation?"

So I scramble up from the floor. With a dozen others, I climb into a police van. When a man raises his handcuffed hands to touch my breasts, I slap them away.

"Keep your hands to yourself!" I shout.

The driver shouts at me to be quiet.

That is how I am transported from temporary lockup to this prison, where I now live.

PT SIR

THE PLAYGROUND IS A RECTANGLE OF CONCRETE, surrounded first by a slim row of trees wilting in the sun, then by the five-story building of the school. The physical-training teacher, in collared shirt and ironed pants, his mustache thick as a shoe-brush and his bald pate shiny, stands in the sun and shouts commands for the students to march in rhythm, arms raised in salute, feet landing sharply on the ground.

The girls, his students, are thirteen years old, their skirts down to their knees, bra straps falling off their shoulders, tired socks curling off their shins. Many have cleaned their white sports shoes with a rub of blackboard chalk. Now their backs slouch, and their arms flop when they should be rigid as blades.

"Haven't you seen," PT Sir scolds as he walks down their rows, "the soldiers' procession on TV? You should look exactly like that!"

Republic Day, the national holiday celebrating the country's constitution, is coming up, and this will not do. The students' parade, the most patriotic performance on this patriotic occasion, is PT Sir's responsibility. It is the one time in all the school year when he, this odd teacher who teaches not geography or mathematics or chemistry, not even home science, showcases his work. Well, he thinks meanly about himself, that is other than all the times he steps up during assembly to fix a malfunctioning microphone, the only man at this girls' school called on for handiwork.

"Quiet!" he scolds when murmurs arise from the girls. "Be serious!"

The class falls silent. Girls look at the ground, laughter suppressed in their mouths.

Off to the side, two girls sit in the shade of a tree and giggle. At the beginning of class, they had come up to him and each whispered in his ear, "Sir, I have got my period. Can I please be excused?"

PT Sir thinks, but is not sure, that they perhaps had their periods last week also. Frowning, he removes a handkerchief from his breast pocket and wipes the sweat off his head, his forehead, his nose. What else can he do?

*

A FEW NIGHTS LATER, on TV, a banner flashes *Breaking news! Breaking news!*

The host of the show walks down the corridors of a newsroom and, pen in hand, announces that a young woman has been arrested in connection with the train bombing. Her name is Jivan. Last name currently unknown.

PT Sir slams his after-dinner dish of sweets on

the table and lunges for the remote. At the sound, his wife emerges from the kitchen, asking, "What happened?"

He raises a finger to his lips, and presses his thumb down on the volume button until sound fills the room. He leans so far forward his face is no more than a few inches from the screen. There, in a video clip being played and replayed, among the jostle of policemen and reporters, is that face, that poorly made plait, that scar on the chin, elements of a person he knows, or knew. Now the girl keeps a hand on her back, like an elderly lady who aches. PT Sir's mustache nearly falls off his face. "Look at this," he whispers to his wife. "Just look."

"Do you know her?" says his wife. "How do you know her?"

"This young woman, all of twenty-two years old," yells a reporter standing in the middle of a lane, curious onlookers crowding into the frame, "was arrested from the slum where I am standing right now. It's the Kolabagan slum, that's right, the Kolabagan slum next to the Kolabagan railway station, where the train was brutally attacked six days ago, killing one hundred and twelve people. In that attack, as we know—"

PT Sir presses a button and the channel changes. Jivan appears once more, a camera zooming in on her face.

"This Muslim woman is charged with *assisting* terrorists who plotted this heinous attack—"

"She has been booked under a very serious crimes

against the nation charge *and* a sedition charge, which is highly unusual—"

"She allegedly made contact with a known re-cruiter for a terrorist cell on Facebook—"

PT Sir presses a button and the channel flips again.

"Why did she bear so much hatred in her heart for her own country? Sociology professor Prakash Mehra is joining us to talk about the alienated youth, and how the Internet—"

PT Sir watches until his eyes smart. He watches until he has seen every bit of footage and analysis available. Outside, the din of car horns.

*

IT WAS NOT SO long ago that Jivan was his student. When she started, one of the school's charity stu-dents, as they were bluntly called, she had never seen a basketball in her life. But the rules were intuitive, and she played with energy, her legs uninhibited, her arms flung, her mouth open in laughter. Jivan scared the others. The aggressive game of kabaddi came to her naturally, and she was perhaps his only student who was disappointed when he asked them to play mild dodgeball.

PT Sir understood, from the fervor with which she played, and how she responded to compliments with a close-mouthed smile, that she needed this class in a way the other girls did not. So he pardoned her soiled skirt. He forgave her old shoes.

Once, when she fainted in the heat of the playground, he took it as his opening to offer her a banana. After that, every now and then, he gave her a sandwich from his own tiffin box, or an apple. Once, a bag of chips. She didn't get enough to eat, he worried. He couldn't have his prize student falling sick. He already had her in mind for march-past at school functions, for training so she could play basketball, or even football, at the city level. She could grow up to be an athlete, like him. Not once had he come across a student of his who showed real promise in his field, until Jivan.

Then, after the class ten board exams, she left school. He never knew why. He understood it to be a matter of school fees. But she offered him no explanation, never acknowledged how he had gone out of his way to support her. A small thing, but he found it rude.

Well, was it a small thing?

When he thinks about it, an old anger flickers to life. He had begun to dream of her as a mentee, but she had not considered him a mentor. She had considered him perhaps no more than a source of occasional free food. She had fooled him.

The TV plays, indifferent to its tired viewer.

"What happened to make this ordinary young woman, Jivan is her name, a terrorist? What led her down the path of anti-national activity, bringing her into alliance with a terrorist group and conspiring to bring down the government? After the break—"

He cannot believe what she has gone on to do.

His nerves thrum. His life is just the same, and yet this proximity to disaster electrifies PT Sir.

Now he knows, there *was* something wrong with Jivan the whole time. There *was* something wrong in her thinking. Or else she would never have left without telling him, a teacher who cared for her, farewell, and thank you.

JIVAN

THIS MORNING, AFTER UMA MADAM, THE CHIEF guard of the women's prison, wakes us up, I find Yashwi in the courtyard. Yashwi, in clean yellow salwar kameez, who has robbed ten or twelve houses. In one of them she left a grandfather tied up so tight he suffocated. But she is a nice girl, always smiling.

She pumps the tube well for me, hopping up, then crouching down with her weight on the lever as water falls like stones into my cupped hands. With the cold water, pulled from reserves deep underground, a taste of minerals on my lips, I wash my face.

When my eyes feel fresh and new, we join the crowd on the other side of the courtyard for our hunks of bread. There is a fist's scoop of potato on top, and a glass of tea ladled from a bucket. I eat, standing on the side, looking to see if anybody is getting more than me. It has happened. I am ready to fight if it happens again.

But the women are in the haze of sleep, the sky is just turning to morning, and the green algae on the ground are damp under my feet. It is as peaceful as it gets in a cage.

After breakfast, we gather in the TV room. Beside me sits Nirmaladi, dupatta drawn over her head, a corner of cloth clenched in her teeth. She sucks the cloth like a baby at a nipple. She used to work as a cook in the outside world, until she accepted twenty thousand rupees for putting rat poison in a family's lunch. Behind me is one-eyed Kalkidi, half of her face burned, laughing hard when I turn to look, the gaps in her teeth showing. Her husband threw acid on her but, somehow, she is the one in jail. These things happen when you are a woman.

Rumors drift. Among us some have killed a child in bed, or slit the throat of an abusive husband. A few things I know, a few things I don't want to know.

On TV, our favorite drama plays: *Why Won't Mother-in-Law Love Me?*

My first day inside, there was an episode of this endless show playing. Here in this TV room, I asked questions: "Listen, sister, did you keep the court-appointed lawyer? Or did you find a better one? How did you pay for your own lawyer?"

I spoke, but it was as if I had said nothing.

All faces were turned to the TV.

What was this place? Before I knew it, I was say-ing, "I am innocent, I swear I didn't—"

Some women turned. Their faces, with jutting teeth, earlobes slit from years of wearing hoops—so human, yet each one a stranger to me—made me feel that I knew nobody in the world.

I cried. I was a child.

Everyone stopped watching TV then, and turned to watch me. The woman with patches of light and dark skin, a kind of leader in the prison, I knew even then, got up from her position on the floor within licking distance of the TV, and came waddling to me. I had heard she was the one who arranged an upgrade from a black-and-white to a color TV. Americandi, American sister, as she was called for her pink skin, took my chin in her hands. She was gentle as a mother. I felt a moment of relief, assurance that made me wipe my tears. Then she slapped me. Her hand, tough as hide, struck my ear and left it whining.

"Blind or what?" she said. "Can't you see we're watching TV?"

Now I watch TV, openmouthed like the others. More than the show, it is the world I watch. A traffic light, an umbrella, rain on a windowsill. The simple freedom of crossing a street.

*

BEFORE I LIVED HERE, I was a working woman. I had a job at a big shop, where we sold clothes—Indian, Western—suitcases, perfumes, wristwatches, even a few books that customers flipped through and put back on the shelves. Day after day I worked my long shifts, keeping stacks of clothes folded and tidy, bringing different sizes to ladies who yelled from the fitting room. I looked at them when they weren't looking at me—their shiny hair, pedicured feet. Their purses with little plastic cards, sources of endless money. I wanted all that too.

They say the recruiter offered me money, plenty of money, to help them navigate the unmarked lanes of the slum, to bring supplies of kerosene to the train.

I live—I lived—in the Kolabagan slum, near the Kolabagan railway station, with my mother and father. Our house, one room with two brick walls and two walls of tin and tarp, was behind a garbage dump, a dump that was so big and occupied by so many crows screaming *kaw kaw* from dawn to night, it was famous. I would say, "I live in the house behind the dump," and everybody would know where I meant. You could say I lived in a landmark building.

A hijra called Lovely, who went around blessing children and newlyweds, lived in the Kolabagan slum too, and some evenings I taught her English. It began as a compulsory school program where each student had to teach the alphabet to an illiterate person. But we continued long after the school graded me on it. Lovely believed she would have a better life someday, and so did I. The path began with *a b c d*. Cat, bat, rat. English is the language of the modern world. Can you move up in life without it? We kept going.

And I was moving up. So what if I lived in only a half-brick house? From an eater of cabbage, I was becoming an eater of chicken. I had a smartphone with a big screen, bought with my own salary. It was a basic smartphone, bought on an installment plan, with a screen which jumped and credit which I filled when I could. But now I was connected to a world bigger than this neighborhood.

*

ON MY WAY TO my job in the kitchen, I peep in the door of the pickle-making room, where six women prepare lime and onion pickles to sell outside. For years, the space was no more than an accidental warehouse of broken goods, until Americandi, our local entrepreneur, set up this operation from which the prison makes petty cash. Now the room is painted and lit, tables covered with jars, the air smelling of mustard. When she sees me, Monalisa takes off her glove to hand me a triangle of lime peel, dark and sour. A few days ago I helped her daughter learn the Bengali alphabet: *paw phaw baw bhaw maw.* The fragrance of the pickled lime makes my tongue water. The salt and acid play on my tongue, and I chew the sourness down.

PT SIR

AT THE END OF A SCHOOL DAY, WHEN THE BOTTOMS of his trousers are soiled, PT Sir holds his bag in his armpit and exits the building. Outside, the narrow lane is crowded with schoolgirls who part for him. Now and then a student calls, "Good afternoon, sir!"

PT Sir nods. But these girls, to whom he taught physical training just hours before, have hiked up their skirts and coiled their hair into topknots. Their fingers are sticky with pickled fruit. They are talking about boys. He can no longer know them, if he ever did.

When the lane opens up onto the main road, PT Sir is startled by a caravan of trucks roaring past. Three and four and five rush by in a scream of wind. Young men sit in the open truck beds, their faces skinny and mustached, their hands waving the saffron flags of ardent nationalism. One young man tucks his fingers in his mouth and whistles.

*

AT THE TRAIN STATION, PT Sir stands at his everyday spot, anticipating roughly where a general compartment door will arrive. He is leaning to look down the tracks when an announcement comes over the speakers. The train will be thirty minutes late.

"Thirty minutes meaning one hour minimum!" complains a fellow passenger. This man sighs, turns around, and walks away. PT Sir takes out his cell phone, a large rectangle manufactured by a Chinese company, and calls his wife.

"Listen," he says, "the train is going to be late."

"What?" she shouts.

"Late!" he shouts back. "Train is late! Can you hear?"

After the terrorist attack on the train, just a few weeks ago, the word "train" frightens her. "What happened now?" she says. "Are things fine?"

"Yes, yes! All fine. They are saying 'technical difficulty.'"

PT Sir holds the phone at his ear and surveys the scene in front. Passengers arrive, running, then learn about the delay and filter away. To those who spread out the day's newspaper on the floor and relax on it, a girl sells salted and sliced cucumber. In his ear, PT Sir's wife says, "Fine, then. Can you bring a half kilo of tomatoes? There is that market just outside your station."

A spouse always has ideas about how you should spend your time. Couldn't he have enjoyed thirty minutes to himself, to drink a cup of tea and sit on the platform?

PT Sir goes to look for tomatoes. Outside the station, on the road where taxis and buses usually honk and curse, nearly scraping one another's side mirrors, all traffic has halted. Motorcyclists use their feet to push forward. PT Sir learns, from a man who grinds tobacco in his palm, that there is a Jana Kalyan (Well-being for All) Party rally, in the field nearby. It is the biggest opposition party in the state. Film star Katie Banerjee is speaking at the rally.

Katie Banerjee! Now, PT Sir thinks, is it better to spend twenty minutes looking for tomatoes, or catching a glimpse of the famous Katie? Tomatoes can be found anywhere. In fact, tomatoes can be bought ten minutes from his house at the local market—why doesn't his wife go there?

So he follows the street, which opens up onto a field trampled free of grass. The crowd, a thousand men or more, waves the familiar saffron flags. They whistle and clap. Some men cluster around an enterprising phuchka walla, a seller of spiced potato stuffed in crisp shells, who has set up his trade. The scent of cilantro and onion carries. On all the men's foreheads, even the phuchka walla's, PT Sir sees a smear of red paste, an index of worship—of god, of country. The men, marked by the divine, wear pants whose bottoms roll under their feet, and hop up now and then to see what is happening. The stage is far away.

"Brother," he says to a young man. He surprises himself with his friendly tone. "Brother, is it really Katie Banerjee up there?"

The young man looks at him, hands PT Sir a small party flag from a grocery store bag full of them, and calls a third man. "Over here, come here!" he yells. Soon that man rushes over, holding a dish of red paste. He dips his thumb in the paste and marks PT Sir's forehead, drawing a red smear from brow to hairline. All PT Sir can do is accept, a child being blessed by an elder.

Thus marked, party flag in his hand, PT Sir steps forward to hear better. Onstage, it is indeed movie star Katie Banerjee, dressed in a starched cotton sari. She too is marked by holy red paste on her forehead, PT Sir sees. Her speech drawing to a close, she raises both hands in a namaste. "You all have come from far districts of the state," she says. "For that you have my thanks. Go home safely, carefully."

The microphone crackles. The crowd roars.

When the star leaves the stage, her place at the microphone is occupied by the second-in-command of the party. Bimala Pal, no more than five feet two, arrives in a plain white sari, her steel wristwatch flashing in the sun. The crowd quiets for her. PT Sir holds the flag above his head for shade, then tries his small leather bag, which works better.

In the microphone, Bimala Pal cries, her words echoing over the speakers: "We will seek justice . . . ice! For the lives lost in this cowardly . . . ardly attack . . . tack on the train . . . train! I promise you . . . you!"

After a minute of silence for the lost souls, she continues, pausing for the echoes to fade, "Where the current government is not able to feed our people!

Jana Kalyan Party—your idle government's hard-working opposition!—has provided rice to fourteen districts for three rupees per kilo! We are inviting plastics and cars, factories which will bring at least fifteen thousand jobs—"

While PT Sir watches, a man wearing a white undershirt pulls himself up, or is pushed up by the crowd, onto the hood of a jeep far ahead. PT Sir had not noticed the jeep until now, but there it is, a vehicle in the middle of the field, still a distance from the stage. The man stands on the hood of the car, survey-ing the raised arms, the open mouths and stained teeth. Then he climbs onto the roof of the car, the car now rocking from the crowd shoving and slamming, their fury and laughter landing on the polished body of the vehicle.

"Fifteen thousand jobs!" they chant. "Fifteen thou-sand jobs!"

Whether they are excited or merely following in-structions from party coordinators is hard to tell. A few TV cameras will pick this up, no doubt.

"We know that you are sacrificing every day!" Bi-mala Pal calls, shouting into the microphone. "And for what? Don't you deserve more opportunities? This party is standing with you to gain those jobs, every rupee of profit that you are owed, every day of school for your children!" Bimala Pal pumps a fist in the air.

PT Sir watches, electricity coursing through him despite himself. Here, in the flesh, are the people of the hinterland about whom he has only seen features on TV. He knows a few things about them: Not only is there no work in their village, there is not even a paved road! Not only is the factory shut down, but the company guard is keeping them from selling the scrap metal!

"Remember that this nation belongs to *you*, not to the rich few in their high-rises or the company bosses in their big cars, but *you*!" Bimala Pal wraps up. "Vande Mataram!"

Praise to the motherland!

The man at the top of the car repeats, screaming, "Vande Mataram!"

PT Sir might have thought that this man, along with hundreds of others, had been trucked here from a village, his empty belly lured by a free box of rice and chicken, his fervor purchased for one afternoon. He might have thought that, for these unemployed men, this rally is more or less a day's job. The party is feeding them when the market is not.

But the man's cries make the hairs on PT Sir's arm stand up, and what is false about that?

The man on the car lifts his shirt and reveals, tucked in the waistband of his trousers, wrapped in a length of cloth, a dagger. He holds the handle and lifts it high in the air, where the blade catches the sun. Below him, surrounding the car, a man dances, then another, and another, a graceless dance of feeling.

The dagger stays up in the air, itself a sun above the field, and PT Sir looks at it, frozen in alarm and excitement. How spirited this man is, with his climb atop a jeep like a movie hero, with his dagger and his dancing. How different from all the schoolteachers PT Sir knows. How free.

*

WHEN THE MEN BEGIN to tire, a coordinator announces, "Brothers and sisters! There are buses! To take you home! Please do not rush! Do not stampede! Everyone will be taken home free of charge!"

PT Sir returns to the train station. He has missed the delayed train, and when the next one comes, he finds an aisle seat, tucking his behind, the fifth, into a seat meant for three. The soles of his feet itch, reminding him they have been bearing his weight for much of the day. Somebody shoves past, dragging a sack over his toes. The person is gone before PT Sir can say anything. A woman then stands beside him, her belly protruding at his ear, and her purse threatening to strike him in the face at any moment. In this crowd, a muri walla, a puffed rice seller, makes his way. "Muri, muri!" he calls. The coach groans.

"Today out of all days!" comes the woman's loud voice above his head. "First the delay, now there is no place to stand, and you have to sell muri here?"

"Harassment, that's what this is," says a voice from somewhere behind PT Sir. "This commute is nothing less than daily harassment!"

"Here, here, muri walla," somebody objects. "Give me two."

"And one here!" someone else calls.

The muri walla mixes mustard oil, chopped tomato

and cucumber, spiced lentil sticks, and puffed rice in a tin. He shakes a jar of spices upside down. Then he pours the muri into a bowl made of newsprint.

PT Sir's stomach growls. He lifts his buttocks to try to reach his wallet.

"And one muri this way!" he says. "How much?"

The muri walla makes him a big bowl, heaping at the top.

"Don't worry," he says, handing the bowl to PT Sir. "For you, no charge."

"No charge?" says PT Sir. He laughs, holding the bowl, unsure whether it is truly his to eat. Then he remembers: the red mark on his forehead, the party flag in his lap. PT Sir feels the other passengers staring at him. They must be thinking, who is this VIP?

*

AT HOME, AFTER DINNER, PT Sir sits back in his chair, gravy-wet fingers resting atop his plate, and tells his wife, "Strange thing happened today. Are you listening?"

His wife is thin and short, her hair plaited such that it needs no rubber band at its taper. When she looks at him from her chair, it appears she has forgiven him for the forgotten tomatoes.

Something has happened at the school, she thinks. A man teaching physical training to a group of girls, all of whom are growing breasts, their bellies cramping during menstruation, their skirts stained now and then. A bad situation is bound to arise.

"What happened?" she says fearfully.

"There was a Jana Kalyan rally in the field behind the station," he begins, "then one man climbed on a car—understand? *Climbed on top of a car*—and took out. . . . Tell me what he took out!"

"How will I know?" she says. When she bites into a milk sweet, white crumbs fall on her plate. "Gun, or what?"

"Dagger!" he says, disappointed. The truth is always modest. He goes on, "But Katie Banerjee was there—"

"Katie Banerjee!"

"Then Bimala Pal also was there. Say what you like about her, she is a good orator. And she was saying some correct things, you know. Her speech was good."

His wife's face sours. She pushes back her chair and its legs scrape the floor. "Speech sheech," she says. "She is pandering to all these unemployed men. This is why our country is not going anywhere."

"They are feeding a lot of people with discounted rice," he says. "And they are going to connect two hundred villages, two hundred, to the electricity grid in two years—"

"You," says his wife, "believe everything."

PT Sir smiles at her. When she disappears into the kitchen, he gets up and washes his hands clean of turmeric sauce, then wipes them on a towel that was once white.

He understands how his wife feels. If you only watch the news on TV, it is easy to be skeptical. But what is so wrong about the common people caring about their jobs, their wages, their land? And what, after all, is so wrong about him doing something different from his schoolteacher's job? Today he did something patriotic, meaningful, bigger than the disciplining of cavalier schoolgirls—and it was, he knows as he lies in bed, no sleep in his humming mind, exciting.

JIVAN

IN THE DAYS-OLD PAPERS THAT MAKE IT TO THE prison, they write versions of my life. They report that I grew up in Sealdah, Salpur, Chhobigram. My father, they share, has polio, cancer, an amputated limb. He used to cook food in a hotel; no, he used to be a municipal clerk; no, in truth he used to be a meter reader for the electricity supply company. They have not found out about my mother's breakfast business, because they write that she is a housewife, when they mention her at all.

"Look," I say to Americandi, who is my cellmate because, I learned, she demanded to be housed with the famous terrorist. "*Desher Potrika* says I used to work at a call center, and they have pictures of somebody! Somebody else on the back of a motorcycle with a man. I have never even been on a motorcycle."

It is midday, after bath time, and my cellmate has hiked up her sari to her thighs and is giving herself a massage, running her fingers up and down calves. Her veins are crooked, like flooding rivers.

"Reporters write anything," she says. "Take my case, where I said—"

But I don't want to hear about her.

"They hear something in the street," I say. "Then they write it down."

"They work on deadlines," she says. "If they miss their deadlines, they are fired. Who has time to ask questions?"

"And it says here, listen," I continue, " 'An Internet cafe operator in the neighborhood said Jivan would often make calls to Pakistan numbers.' Why are they lying about me?"

Americandi looks at me. "You know, many people don't believe you. Myself, I heard everything. There was kerosene in your home. You were at the train station. You were friends with the recruiter. Did you do it?" She sighs. "But somehow, I don't see you as a bad person."

A sob rises thick in my throat.

"Listen," she says. "I am not supposed to tell you, but you know reporters are beating down the gates trying to get an interview with you?"

I wipe my eyes and blow my nose. "Which paper?" I say.

"The Times of India! Hindustan Times! The Statesman!" she says. "Name any paper. All are offering money, so much money, just for one interview with you. That's what I heard. But Uma madam is forced to say no to all of them. There is pressure from above."

"It is my right to talk to them!" I shout.

Americandi makes as if to slap me. "Keep your voice down!" she hisses. "This is why I shouldn't be nice to anyone in this rotten place."

She picks a sari from the stack of four that I have washed and folded for her. She winds the sari about herself. She tucks in the top of the pleats. "You have the *right*?" she says, kicking a leg under the fabric to order the pleats. Under a smile, she buries all else she meant to say.

"I want to talk to them," I say softly. "What is Gobind doing for me anyway? I have not seen him in days. Not once has he called me."

If only I could speak to a newspaper reporter, a TV camera, wouldn't they understand? Every day I bear this dark corridor with its rustle of insects' wings, the drip of a leak which conveys news of the rains, the plaster on the ceiling swelling like a cloud. Days have turned into weeks, and still I kneel by the gutter in the back, washing Americandi's nighties by hand, the smell of iron rising where we all wash our monthly cloths. I have been a fool to wait for Gobind's plan, I see. He may be my court-appointed lawyer, but he is no advocate of mine.

This is why, I think, we are all here. Take Americandi. She pushed a man who was trying to snatch her necklace on the street. The man fell, and struck his head on the pavement. He went into a coma. The court charged Americandi, and here she is, a decade or more into confinement that never ends. If she had received a chance to tell her story, how might her life have been?

*

THE NEXT MORNING, Americandi gathers her thin towel, rough as a pumice stone, and a bottle of perfumed liquid soap she guards with her life. She is off to take a bath.

"Listen," I say, while the day is new and Americandi's mood unspoiled, "will you do one thing for me?"

I hold up the newspaper I have been looking at.

"Will you send word to this reporter?" I unfold the newspaper, *Daily Beacon,* and look at the name Purnendu Sarkar. "Ask this Purnendu Sarkar to come? My mother said he visited her. He was helpful."

Americandi looks about for her shower slippers.

"Good plan!" she says, mocking. "Why should I be bothered?"

She waits, and turns to me. I have one moment of her attention, no more.

"The money," I tell her. "What they offer for an interview. You just said, they are offering a lot? You can take it all. What can the courts do if the media does not—"

"You really love lecturing," says Americandi. "Did you say *all* the money?"

"Every rupee."

"When did you become such a rich person?" she says.

PT SIR

NOTHING GOOD COMES OF CONTACTING THE POLICE. Everybody knows that. If you catch a thief, you are better off beating the man and, having struck fear in his heart, letting him go.

But this is no ordinary thief. This is a woman who attacked a train full of people. She killed, directly or indirectly, more than a hundred people. Now, the TV channels are reporting, she is silent in prison. She has granted no interviews. She has offered no details, and other than a confession, which she insists she was forced to sign, she has shared no information. She is protesting that she is innocent.

The police, desperate for progress, have asked Jivan's friends and associates to step forward. Nobody will be harassed, they have promised. They are only looking for insight into the character of the terrorist, some scrap of information that will crack the case open. The men involved in the case have long slipped across the border and fled. Jivan is the only hope.

So it is that one morning, encouraged by his wife, PT Sir, in fresh clothes, his sparse hair combed, his belly full of breakfast, picks up the phone and calls the local police station. When the superintendent on duty, a man who insists on speaking in English, urges him to come to the station right away, PT Sir does. So consumed is his mind that it is only halfway on his walk to the station that he realizes he is still wearing his house slippers.

JIVAN

WHEN MY MOTHER CAME TO VISIT FOR THE FIRST time, she cried to hand over a tiffin carrier, full of home-cooked food, to the guards. She did it again, and again, hoping the meals would reach me. Then I told her, "Why are you cooking for the guards?"

I watched her cry then, my own eyes dry.

Today, upon my request, she hands me, not cooked food, but a small pouch, knotted shut, filled with golden oil. It is ghee.

"What will you do with this?" she asks.

I tell her.

Then she is gone, all the mothers are gone, and the rest of the day stretches before us. In the court-yard, I see a fight among three women—teeth bared, hair coming unclipped. They scream about a missing milk sweet.

For the rest of the day, we fall and die from know-ing, but never being able to say, especially to our mothers, that the inside of the prison is an unreach-able place. So what if there is a courtyard, and a garden, and a TV room? The guards tell us over and over that we live well, we live better than the trapped souls in the men's prison. Still we feel we are living at the bottom of a well. We are frogs. All we can bear to tell our mothers is "I am fine, I am fine."

We tell them, "I walk in the garden."

"I watch TV."

"Don't worry about me, I am fine."

*

THE KITCHEN, where my work is to make ruti, holds a large grill which allows me to make bread in batches of ten. One woman kneads the dough, one tears balls and flattens them into disks, several roll them flat and round, and I tend them as they're tossed on the grill. When they're done, I lift them with long tongs and flip them onto the stone surface next to the grill. There, a couple of women dust the flour off and stack them.

After making a hundred and twenty pieces of ruti, I pour the ghee on the grill. The scent is the luxury that I imagine sleeping on a bed of feathers must be, or bathing in a tub of milk like the old queens of our country. With my hand, I flip the dough in the pool of clarified butter, and the edges crisp. The bread rises, and its belly gains brown spots.

When I take a plate to Uma madam, she is sitting on a plastic chair in the courtyard, her arms draped on the sides, like the ruler of a meager kingdom. Surrounding her, in tidy rows, inmates eat. She accepts the plate, and looks at me with a sly smile.

"Why this preparation?" she says. "What do you want now?"

She is not angry.

I step back and watch her eat the porota. I hear the shatter of the crisp dough, or maybe I imagine it. She folds the porota around a smear of dal and lifts it to her mouth. I watch like a jackal. My stomach growls.

In the row of seated inmates and their children, a little girl cries. A boy whines for food, though he has just eaten. The children are each given a boiled egg and milk every other day. Other than that, there is no concession made to their growing bodies, their muscles stretching overnight. They eat the same stale curry as the rest of us. The mothers have agitated over this, but who will listen to them?

Uma madam twists around in the chair, spots me, and gives me a thumbs-up. She lifts the plate to show me. She has eaten every bite.

Kneeling at Uma madam's feet, I take the empty plate from her. I can feel the damp algae green my knees.

"So," she says, digging in her teeth with her tongue, "what was this about?"

"I have a brother," I say. "He wants to visit. Can you approve him for my visitors' list? His name is Purnendu Sarkar."

I try to smile. My lips manage it.

"Brother, hmm?" she says. "You never mentioned him. Was he living in a cave until today?"

"No, he was working outside the city—"

When Uma madam stands up, she puts her hands

on her waist and arches her spine. She squints at the sky. With a look of great boredom, she turns to me. "The fewer lies you tell, the better for you. God knows how many lies you tell every day."

Then she is gone, and I am left holding the plate. There is a thin shard of porota sticking to the rim, an airy nothing made of flour. Not even a fly would be nourished by it. I pinch it with my fingers, and put it in my mouth.

LOVELY

EVEN A FUTURE MOVIE STAR IS HAVING TO MAKE
money. One morning my sisters and I are spraying
rose water in our armpits, braiding our hair, putting
bangles on our arms, and together we are going to
bless a newborn. The general public is believing that
we hijras are having a special telephone line to god.
So if we bless, it is like a blessing straight from god.
At the door of the happy family, I am rattling the lock
thuck thuck thuck.

"Give, mother," we are calling so that our voices
can be heard deep within the big house. When nobody is coming, I am stepping back and looking up
at a window. It is a big house, and the window is
covered by a lace curtain.

"Mother!" I am calling. "Let us see the baby,
come."

Finally the door in front of us is opening, and
the mother, wearing a nightie that goes only to her
calves, her oily hair sticking to her scalp, her eyes
looking like she has seen battle, is holding the baby
and coming out. Poor woman is yawning like a hip-

popotamus. I am feeling that maybe I can make the
mother cheer up, along with the baby.

So I am taking the baby in my arms, inhaling the
milk scent of his skin. My eyes are falling in love
with those soft folds in his wrists, the plump inside
of his elbows. The others are clapping above the baby,
singing, "God give this child a long life, may he never
suffer the bite of an ant! God give this child a happy
life, may he never suffer a lack of grains!"

The baby is looking surprised, with those big eyes.
Maybe he is never coming out on the street before,
never feeling the smoke and dust. For sure he is
never seeing a group of hijras in our best clothes!
He is screaming. His little mouth is opening to show
pink gums and pink tongue, and he is screaming in
my arms. He is a little animal. We are laughing. He is
going to be fine, I am thinking, because he is having
no defects, unlike myself.

The mother is looking harassed, and taking the
baby inside. We are waiting for the sound of a drawer
opening, some cash being counted by mother and
father. But what is this, she is going inside a room,
where a tap is running and water is falling. From
here, over all the sounds of the street, I am hearing
one sound clearly: She is washing her hands. She is
washing her hands of us.

Meanwhile, the father is coming out in shorts and
giving Arjuni Ma, our hijra house's guru, three thousand whole rupees. He is sliding his glasses down
his nose and looking at us from the top. One of my
sisters is flirting with him for an old microwave or

old TV. He is looking unhappy and pleading, "Where am I having so much, sister? Look at me. New baby and all."

Me, I am only trying to see what the mother is doing behind him, in the dark corridor, her hands so, so clean.

*

IT IS NOT NEW, this insult. But it is not old. I am leaving the group and hurrying to the sweet shop down the street. Inside there is running a long glass case holding trays full of sweets. The pyramids of sweets, some dry, some soaking in syrup, are tempting me. There is brown pantua, fried and syrupy; there is white chomchom, so sweet your tongue will be begging for salt; there are milky and dry kalakand; and there is my favorite, kheer kodom. I am smelling the whole case from where I am standing, believe me. I am feeling the flavor of the flies buzzing over the sweets, and how some of the old sweets are beginning to sour in the hot day.

"How much is this?" I am saying. "And how much this one?"

The man behind the counter is grumbling. He is unhappy that he is having to serve me, I know. Finally I am getting one small roshogolla, ten rupees. The man is giving it to me in a small bowl woven with dried leaves. I am lifting the bowl to my forehead. I am giving thanks. It is no small thing to buy a sweet, and that is enough today. That is how my life is going forward—some insult in my face, some sweet in my mouth.

Someday, when I am a movie star, that mother will be regretting that she washed me off her hands.

*

IN THE EVENING, when my sisters are coming to my house, wearing nice saris for their outing, mosquitoes the size of birds are flying in happily also. One of my sisters is saying, "Did the police ask you anything?"

It is true that Jivan was teaching me English, so for sure the police will be coming to interrogate me. How come they are not coming yet?

In the corner of the room, hanging from a nail, is a coil of cables. One of my sisters is pulling a line and plugging it into the boxy TV on the floor. After she is slapping the top of the TV, it is waking up. That classic movie *A Match Made by God* is starting.

While the songs are playing, Arjuni Ma is raising her notebook close to her old eyes and reading what we have earned this week. Five thousand for a marriage, three thousand for a baby blessing. A few hundred rupees from the train.

My mind is somewhere else. Who is liking the police? Nobody. But I am also hoping that they are coming and I am getting a chance to tell them that Jivan was teaching me English. Impossible that Jivan is a criminal. Cannot be. I am wanting to tell the police this.

"When they come," Arjuni Ma is telling me later, "be careful when you talk to them. Maybe it is better that you try to avoid them."

We are all knowing what is happening to hijras who are displeasing police, like Laddoo, our young hijra sister who was going to the police to report harassment from a constable, and was herself put in the lockup. There she is staying for days and days. Many years ago I would have been asking why is this happening? But now I am knowing that there is no use asking these questions. In life, many things are happening for no reason at all. You might be begging on the train and getting acid thrown on your face. You might be hiding in the women's compartment for safety and getting kicked by the ladies.

I was almost being arrested one time also. A constable named Chatterjee was catching me when I was begging near the traffic light. He was saying to me, "Now you are trying to do this nonsense in my area?"

"What?" I was challenging him. "I can't stand on the road?" I was speaking like a heroine. I was new. I was not knowing.

Anything could have happened. But he was a reasonable man. He was letting me go after I was buying him a single cigarette and lighting it for him.

JIVAN

IN PRISON, OUR MAIN ACTIVITY IS WAITING. I WAIT for Americandi to get confirmation from the journalist that he will come, and to see if Uma madam will look the other way. In the complete black of night, I wonder if there are other ways. If my hands were spades, they would burrow from my cell to beyond the garden wall, where buses race, where beggars loiter, where women wearing sunglasses buy chop-cutlet for evening tea.

In the morning, I stand in line for breakfast. A rumor goes around: Sonali Khan, the famous film producer whose name every household is knowing, was spotted in the booking room. Everybody cheers. What did *she* do? we wonder. Did she hit somebody with her car? Did she hide some money in Switzerland?

"You all," says Americandi, ahead of me in line, "don't know anything. It's that rhino."

The film producer once shot, from the safety of a jeep, an endangered rhino. The ghost of this rhino has caught up with her. She is finally being punished for it. Now she will live with us, and tell us all about the cinema.

Yashwi says, "Definitely we will get a new TV, then!"

"What's wrong with this TV?" snaps Americandi. "If you don't like it, see if you can arrange for a new TV for yourself."

"No, I mean . . ." Yashwi looks at her feet. I know she dreams of a TV whose pictures will not jump, whose remote control will work.

Komla, who once robbed a family, striking with an iron rod a mother who was left paralyzed, begins to salivate thinking of the meals in store.

"Chicken curry," she calls, turning her head up and down the line for the benefit of all, "for sure we will get chicken curry. Regularly!"

She sticks a finger in her ear and shakes it vigorously to scratch an unreachable itch. "Maybe mutton also, who knows?"

I listen, believing myself far away.

When we have returned to our cells, and Uma madam comes on her round, I catch her eye.

"Have you put my brother on the list?" I ask her.

She looks at me blankly and continues on her path, the ring of keys singing at her hips. But Americandi, greedy for the two hundred thousand rupees the *Daily Beacon* has promised for an interview with me, leaps up and stands at the gate.

"Uma," she calls. "Come here."

Down the corridor, the constant chatter and clang of our prison pauses.

There is a long silence while Uma madam saunters back. "What did you say?" she says softly. "Am I your best friend? Talk to me with respect."

Somebody in a neighboring cell whistles.

"What is this, TV hour!" somebody else comments.

"Okay, Uma *madam*," my cellmate says. "This poor girl," she continues, pouting, in a voice loud enough to carry down the corridor, "got ghee from her mother to cook for you. And you won't let her see her own brother? Shame! How must her mother be feeling?"

"Let her see her boyfriend, for god's sake!" somebody says, laughing.

Uma madam stands still. I watch from behind Americandi.

"Don't interrupt my round again," Uma madam says quietly. Then she is gone.

*

THE WEEKS PASS and nothing changes. In the courtyard? No Sonali Khan. In the TV room? The same old TV. Every week the women pin their hopes on a different day—surely she will be transferred here this Sunday, or next Thursday. Then we hear that Sonali Khan is being kept under house arrest, which means that she lives, as before, in her own house. Even the meaning of "prison" is different for rich people. Can you blame me for wanting, so much, to be—not even rich, just middle class?

PT SIR

THE SECOND TIME PT SIR GOES TO A JANA KALYAN
Party rally, he stands close to the stage.

"You can see with your own eyes," Bimala Pal continues, "what this party—"

The microphone screeches. Bimala Pal takes a step back. The crowd roars and waves tiny flags. PT Sir waves his flag, saved from the previous rally.

"What this party brings to districts across the state," Bimala Pal says. "The auto parts factory—"

The microphone screeches again, and the crowd murmurs. Some cover their ears with their palms.

"The factory employing three! thousand!—"

Screech. This time, Bimala madam looks about with a stern face for a technician. Behind her a number of assistants dash about, looking for the sound guy, who has probably wandered off to smoke a cigarette. The crowd stirs in boredom.

In a mad and decisive moment, PT Sir marches forward, angling his body sideways and holding an arm out in front of him.

"Side," he calls, "side!" He climbs the steps to the

stage two at a time, assuring Bimala Pal's bodyguards that he intends only to fix the microphone. He wiggles the cord and tests the jack, then moves the microphone farther away from the speaker. He steps up and says, "Testing, testing."

His voice rings out clean and sharp over the crowd.

PT Sir's drumming heart calms.

Bimala Pal resumes her speech, and from a plastic chair somebody offers him at the back of the stage, PT Sir looks out over the vast number of men who have gathered. It is many stadiums' worth of men, their heads like the bulbs of ants. These are not the spoiled and lazy students who occupy his days, nor the teacher aunties who proceed as a horde after school to watch Bengali detective films and eat Chinese noodles. When has he ever been among so many patriots, men who are invested in the development of the nation, who are here in a field listening to an intellectual lecture rather than at home, under a sheet, taking a nap?

After Bimala Pal closes her speech, she comes around to the back of the stage, and thanks him. PT Sir jumps up and folds his hands in greeting.

"I am just a schoolteacher." PT Sir gestures down the road. "At the S. D. Ghosh Girls' School."

Bimala Pal leans in.

"*That* school?"

"Yes, that one," PT Sir says. The terrorist's school. "In my school functions I set up the microphone, so . . ."

Both turn to look at the microphone. It is turned off and silent on its stand. Somebody has garlanded it.

"Well, teacher sir," says Bimala Pal, "it is our good fortune that you came."

Later PT Sir's wife will say, "*That* was a scolding for coming to the stage! Don't you know that politicians always say the opposite of what they mean? It is called diplomacy."

But PT Sir is glad. An esteemed public figure, taking note of him! A gathering of assistants behind Bimala Pal nods and voices its agreement.

Bimala Pal draws the anchal of her sari around her shoulders, and continues, "We need educated people like you to support our party. More educated people must care about what is happening in our state, in our country. So to see a teacher like you at our rally makes me glad."

PT Sir opens his mouth to say something. He must clarify that he teaches physical education. He is not the kind of teacher she imagines, he is only—

A boy appears with dishes of samosas, and after that there is chicken biryani for all. The men in the fields have received, away from the glare of a TV camera, and distributed from the rear of a discreet van, their dinner boxes of biryani too. They take their boxes quietly and disperse.

But there is a problem. There are more men in the field than boxes of biryani. A scuffle breaks out. The man handing out boxes of biryani immediately closes the back doors of the van. Bimala Pal and her lackeys turn to look, and PT Sir looks too.

A man, not too far from the stage, points his finger at another. "This one is taking three boxes! He is hiding them in his bag!"

That man demands, "Who are you calling a thief?"

An open palm slaps a face, a leg kicks a leg.

Bimala Pal has slipped away, cupping a hand around her mouth on her phone, occupied by a more pressing matter. One of her assistants turns to PT Sir and jokes, "Well, sir, look at these rowdy children."

The other assistants, young men holding two mobile phones each, wait with hidden smiles to see what the teacher will do.

PT Sir feels the eyes on him. The pressure is subtle but great. He steps up to the edge of the stage, sits on the pads of his feet, and calls, "Brothers, brothers! There is food for all! Why are you fighting like children?"

The men in the crowd look up at him.

"Are you children," PT Sir continues, "that you are spoiling the gathering here with your fight? Do you want to disgrace the party, and our elders who have gathered here, in front of those reporters over there?"

"Who are you?" a man shouts at PT Sir. "Who are you, mister, to tell me what to do?"

But the fight has lost its air. The men separate with some curses. When PT Sir returns to his seat and picks up his box of biryani, one of the assistants stops him.

"Wait, please," he says, "the rice has grown cold by now, wait one minute."

He calls the tea boy—"Uttam!"—and asks him

to bring a "VIP box" right away. A fresh, hot box of biryani, with two pieces of mutton, arrives for PT Sir.

*

"TODAY I AM NOT HUNGRY," PT Sir announces at home. "Today I had biryani with, guess who? Bimala Pal!"

His wife looks up from her phone. In the background, softly, the news plays. PT Sir settles heavily on the sofa, and picks up the remote. He turns up the volume. A reporter shouts: "This alleged terrorist used a very modern way of spreading her anti-national views, find out how she used *Facebook*—"

On another channel, a soft-spoken news host says: "On top of throwing torches at the train, dear viewers, let me tell you all, she was also sharing anti-government views on Facebook, and who knows where else, for *years*—"

"Beware," PT Sir tells his wife. "What all you do on Facebook. It's full of criminals."

"Your head," she says, "is filled with all this. I only look at cooking videos. It's a totally different part of Facebook. People abroad make such nice things, you don't know—like apple pie with ready-made whipped cream! I have never seen such things. The cream comes out of a can."

At bedtime, when they climb under the mosquito net, his wife marvels at the story he has told her. "Imagine that!" she says. "You saving the day at a JKP rally!"

A mosquito has followed them inside the net. It

buzzes near their ears until she locates the mosquito resting on the sheet and smacks her hand down on it. A blot of blood appears, and she carries the corpse of the mosquito off the bed and flings it out of the window.

Then she stands by the window, and pulls the glass closed. She draws the curtain. Only then does she say, "Can I tell you something?"

He waits.

"I don't know about these politicians," she says. "In our country politics is for goons and robbers, you know that."

PT Sir sighs.

His wife continues, "When you do something for them, like you helped them when their technician was not there, they make you feel nice. On a stage, in front of so many people—who wouldn't feel like a VIP? But associating with such people—"

This irritates PT Sir. He lies with his head on his thin pillow and wonders why his wife cannot tolerate something exciting that is happening in his life. She is annoyed, he feels, because he didn't have much of an appetite for the yogurt fish she cooked. She is annoyed because he filled his belly with store-bought biryani. But he is a man! He is a man with bigger capacities than eating the dinner she cooks.

"Well," he says in as calm a voice as he can manage. It is easier in the dark. "Why are you getting worried? I just went to one rally."

She slides back into bed, her silence thick. "You went to two," she says finally. After a pause, she speaks again. "Please, I ask you," she says, "don't go to more rally shally."

PT Sir thinks about this for hours, until deep night has settled into the home, turning their furniture unfamiliar, amplifying a squeak here, a knock there. Somewhere a clock ticks. Far away, an ambulance siren sounds.

JIVAN

THIS VISITING DAY, SEATED ON A BENCH WAITING FOR me, is not my mother but a man. He has a beard, and a cloth bag in his lap. At his feet, a plastic sack which he lifts and hands to me. His soft fingers against mine are a shock.

The bag is heavy. Inside, I see a bunch of bananas, and a packet of cookies.

"You are . . ." I say.

"Purnendu," he says, with no hi or hello. He is gentle, gentler than any reporter I have encountered. "How is your health?" he asks me.

"Fine," I tell him. I look again inside the bag, at the perfectly yellow bananas, no bruises on them that I can see. I want to eat them all, right now.

"Sit," he suggests when I remain standing.

"You are not allowed to take notes," I say, pointing at the pen in his fingers. "Didn't they tell you that?"

"Oh," he says, looking down at the pen in his hand, as if he has just noticed it. He puts it on the bench between us. "Then this is useless," he says, smiling.

There is a joke in his words that I don't catch. Is it a pen, or . . . ?

"Please don't do anything so that they will kick you out," I say. "I want to tell you everything, if you promise to print the truth. The other newspapers are printing rubbish, lies, they know nothing about my story—"

"That's what I do," he says. "Report the truth. That's why I'm here."

He glances at the clock on the wall. The guard on duty stands in a far corner and looks at us.

"Tell me your story," says Purnendu.

*

WHEN I WAS A CHILD, I lived—

Believe me when I say you must understand my childhood to know who I am, and why this is happening to me.

"Tell me one thing first," says Purnendu. "Did you do it?"

I lick my lips. I try to look him in the eye. I shake my head.

*

IN MY VILLAGE, the dust of coal settled in the nooks of our ears, and when we blew our noses it came out black. There were no cows, or crops. There were only blasted pits into which my mother descended with a shovel, rising with a basket of black rock on her head.

"Did you see her working?" Purnendu asks.

"I watched her once," I tell him. "Never again."

It frightened me to see her as a worker. At night I held her palm in my palm. The lines in her hands—lifelines, they call them—were the only skin not blackened.

*

MANY DAYS I WENT to school for the free midday meal of lentils and rice. There were rumors that we would get chicken in the festival season. Somebody said they saw a man ride in the direction of our school on a bicycle weighted with chickens, their legs bound, hanging upside down from the handlebars, all those white hens silent and blinking at the receding path. But that hoped-for bicycle never arrived.

I sat in this class or that class. It did not matter. When the language teacher reappeared after a long absence for her wedding, she chewed a paan stuffed with lime and betel nut, and told us to write our names on the tests. One day, she reminded us, "Stick five rupees to the page if you can."

She would fill in the rest of the test if we did.

Soon, only goats were going to school, leaving pellets on the porch.

*

"TELL ME," I SAY. "How does this sound to you? What kind of start did I get in life?"

Purnendu looks at me and smiles sadly. "Such is our country," he says.

*

THEN THE POLICEMEN CAME to evict us. The company wanted to mine the land on which we lived, rich with coal. Why should the company let some poor people sit and bathe and sleep on top of vast sums of money?

For a week we had saved our shits in plastic bags which we twirled closed, and our urine in soda bottles we capped tight, to make what my mother and father called bombs. The rickshaw Ba occasionally drove, ferrying mine workers, stood outside, its accordion roof folded, blue seat gleaming, and I prayed for mercy—where could he hide a rickshaw?

We waited in our huts, tarp snapping in the wind, our throats parched but nobody willing to leave their house to go to the municipal tap.

The policemen were late.

When they came, they came holding bamboo sticks, followed by the rumble of bulldozers, whose treads I watched, frightened. Mother slapped my head and said, "What are you looking at with your mouth open? Can't you hear I'm calling?"

Hit me again, Mother, I think now. I will bear it like a blessing.

I rubbed my head, and unscrewed my soda bottle a little, so that the cap would fly off midair and spatter the policemen. I threw my urine bombs at them, traces of liquid on my fingers. I untwisted the plastic bags and threw the hard and dry cakes of shit, the dust of our own waste making us sneeze.

The policemen laughed at our poor weaponry. Their bellies, hanging over their belts, quivered. They swung methodically with their bamboo rods, bringing down our asbestos and tarp roofs. They grunted and yelled with the exertion. One gentle policeman lined up the glinting sheets of asbestos against a naked wall, as if somebody would come to collect them.

Soon our houses were exposed to the sun, all lime walls and cracked corners. They looked like we had never lived in them at all.

The sight of our houses, so easily broken, startled me. I knew it would happen, but like this? Kitchens in which we had eaten before a flickering kerosene lamp, rooms in which we had combed each other's hair, all roofless, soon to be crushed into a heap of brick.

News of our bombs had reached the police station, and new policemen arrived, this time wearing helmets and carrying shields of cane which looked like the backs of chairs, meant to deflect knives and stones. They had heard "bombs," they were expecting bombs, and they were angry. But we had no real weapons. We had our bodies and our voices, our saved waste long gone.

When a policeman raised his bamboo stick to strike my mother, she screamed and threw herself at him, her voice strangled and soaring at once, her sari unfurling into the mud and shit at our feet, loose blouse slipping off her shoulders, her face black with rage.

"Leave our houses alone," she screamed. "Where will we live?"

Until then I had naively believed another home would materialize, but in my mother's transformation I saw the truth: We had nowhere to go.

Another policeman held her legs and began dragging her, and I watched in horror until I felt my arms rise and push him away, striking his face so that his spectacles fell and were trampled. My mother scrambled up and retreated, screaming curses until her voice snapped, the thread of it drifting down. In the meantime, somebody had smashed my father's rickshaw. I looked, uncomprehending, at the bent wheels and slashed seat, my father kneeling to reattach, futilely, the cycle chain to the ruined vehicle.

The houses fell. Walls and roofs of our shelter turned enemy, wreckage coming down on our heads, the rising dust making us cough, paint and brick in heaps on the ground. The policemen, finally calm, bamboo limp by their sides, looked frightened. Maybe the houses looked too much like their own. In the end, one policeman pleaded with us, "Orders came from above, sister, what will I do?"

*

"TIME, TIME," CALLS A GUARD. She strides about the room, striking each bench with a stick. Our hour is over.

My brother, Purnendu, stands up and lifts the cloth bag on his shoulder.

"Next week," he says, "and the week after that, and the week after that, for as long as it takes."

His words play in my ears with the sweetness of

a flute. I watch him go, past a door which magically opens for him, and I turn back. Inside, a woman beats her head on the wall. Once, I might have felt that way too, but now I don't. Now I float beside her, her scrape only hers, not mine. I am on my way out. As soon as the newspaper publishes my story, the door will begin to open for me. Where public feeling goes, the court follows. Freedom will result not from boxes of papers and fights over legality but from a national outcry.

I walk past the woman striking her head. A guard appears, and tells the woman, in a tone of boredom, to stop striking her head.

"What are you doing," the guard drones. "Stop it right now."

The woman pauses, turns, and strikes the guard with her head.

"Ooh!" gasps the corridor.

The woman is taken away, screaming, for something they will call treatment.

INTERLUDE

A POLICEMAN FIRED FOR EXCESSIVE VIOLENCE DURING SLUM DEMOLITION HAS A NEW GIG

"HIGHWAY." YOU SEE, THIS IS A FANCY WORD. THIS road is just a road. It runs straight through the forest. It is paved, and in the rains it is potholed. You see the mounds of red soil? Termite hills. There used to be deer, but we haven't seen any all year. So my friends and I, we come usually at night, yes, regularly at night. Ten o'clock, eleven o'clock. After our women and children have gone to sleep.

Me, personally, after I lost my job after that cursed slum demolition, more than a decade ago, I never got a job again. I do some of this, some of that. Some transportation business. Some import-export. Some middleman fees. That's how I manage.

These days, as I was saying, my friends and I come to this highway, and we park in our cars by the side and wait. One time a poor old villager, maybe the village guard, came tottering up to us saying, "What, son, did your car have a breakdown?"

We laughed. "Grandpa," we said. "Have you seen this car? It's from foreign! It doesn't break down!

"You go," we said to him, "go back to sleep. Go."

The old man understood and went away, or else some of our younger brothers were just itching to use their cutlasses for something other than cutting weeds, you know what I am saying?

Gradually a truck came. It had one of the major signs of cow transportation—some liquid dripping from the back. Now, it could be water, okay. But really? It could also be cow urine. It could mean there are cows on that truck, holy mother cows being taken to slaughter by some bastards. We made it our job to stop the slaughter. If we don't defend our nation, our way of life, our holy cow, who will? We waved our flashlights and the driver stopped.

When the truck stopped, our men went around to the sides and hit the truck, *bang bang bang,* so that any cows inside would move. That's how we would know if that truck was carrying cows. We heard nothing. Meanwhile, in front, the driver was yelling, "What are you all doing? This truck has only potatoes! I am taking potatoes to cold storage!"

"So what is the water?" challenged one of our men, holding his cutlass by his side.

"It rained!" shouted the driver. "It didn't rain here?"

Turned out, he was telling the truth. So we let that truck go.

We are moral men. We are principled men.

But let me tell you, there are persons who don't have any respect for our nation. They don't have any respect for mother cow, and they attack her for beef, for leather, all sorts of disgusting things. There is really no place for such persons in our society, don't you think so?

PT SIR

EARLY IN THE MORNING ON REPUBLIC DAY, A HAZE of pollution softens the skyline, and children stand sleepy-eyed before the national flag, singing the anthem. Teachers watching the show hold handkerchiefs on their noses to ward off smog and chill.

When it is time for the students' parade, PT Sir walks down the line of schoolgirls, reminding them to swing their arms high, to beware of limp salutes. He inspects their uniforms: Their white shoes are clean, their fingernails are clipped. He is almost done with his final check when there is a murmur of activity at the school gate. Somebody has arrived.

Leading a small group of people, the principal shows the way to somebody who follows. Then PT Sir sees a familiar saffron scarf hanging loosely about the neck of a woman in a white sari. Bimala Pal shushes his exclamations.

"I had work right next door, I will only stay for two minutes," she says.

A student promptly unfolds a chair in the front,

and a few more for the assistants and bodyguards who follow. Another student is dispatched to buy tea and freshly cooked shingara, pastry filled with spiced potatoes and peas. The principal, too flustered to look for the petty cash box, hands the student money from her own purse.

Bimala Pal protests, "Please, nothing special for me. I have just come to visit, even though your sir did not invite me!"

At this she looks at him, teasing.

PT Sir bites the tip of his tongue and shakes his head. "How would I invite you to such a humble event?" he says.

Rows of teachers and students gape at the VIP visitor, while her bodyguards stand as a wall behind her, sunglasses on their noses, declining the plastic chairs procured for them.

Now, with Bimala Pal seated and a dish of shingara in front of her, an earthen cup of milk tea at her feet, the principal offers, "PT Sir is one of our most valued teachers."

PT Sir looks at her, amazed.

"He is beloved by the students," the principal continues. "Really, it is his hard work that has made this ceremony come together."

PT Sir smiles graciously at the lies, then turns away to help the students begin the parade. The girls march in single file, their knees rising higher at the sight of Bimala Pal, their voices crisply calling out the beat, "One-two-one! One-two-one!"

PT Sir watches as the playground fills with his

students. His back is straight as a rod, a pen smartly tucked into his shirt pocket, his chin held a little higher.

*

AT HOME, PT SIR's wife offers him a paneer kebab, cooked on the stovetop.

"Don't make that face," she says. "Paneer is good for you. With your cholesterol, you should be eating less meat."

So he eats the cubes. They are a bit dry.

"You can't make proper kebab without a tandoor," responds his wife, miffed. "Don't eat it, then."

But he eats. While he eats, he tells her the story of Bimala Pal's visit. How the Jana Kalyan Party's second-in-command came to *his* school to see *his* ceremony.

"You are so easily flattered!" his wife says. "She was coming to see where the terrorist went to school. What else did you think?"

*

ONLY A FEW WEEKS after PT Sir's ego is thus punctured, he comes home from school to find a letter in the mailbox. Inside, on the sofa, when he tears the edge open, he sees an invitation on Jana Kalyan Party letterhead. He jumps up and waves it before his wife, who is seated at the dining table, tucking cheese inside slit chicken breasts.

"Look what has come!" he says. "How did they find my address?"

His wife wipes her hand on her kameez and takes the letter in hand.

"They have their ways," she says with a smile.

To go to this special event, which will be held on a Monday, PT Sir requests a half day off from school.

On the given date, PT Sir rides a train, then a rickshaw, to the Kolabagan slum. He holds his small leather bag on his lap as the rickshaw descends from the main road into the lanes of the slum, jerking and bouncing over potholes, crossing buildings of brick, then half-brick, then tin and tarp. Jivan lived nearby, he knows, so he observes the surroundings all the more keenly. At a corner, before a municipal pump where water spills, men with checkered cloths wrapped around their waists rub their torsos with soap, their heads white with froth and their eyes closed to the street. The rickshaw moves on, the driver's legs pumping. On a rickety bench before a tea shop, customers sitting with ankle resting on knee and drinking from small glasses in their hands look at PT Sir as he passes by.

When the rickshaw deposits PT Sir at his destination, he finds a crowd gathered in front of a primary school. Damaged in the attack at the railway station nearby, the school building has been renovated over the past months, and is being reopened with great ceremony by the Jana Kalyan Party. The school is no more than a five-room shed. Murals on the exterior walls show a lion, a zebra, and a giraffe strolling alongside a herd of rabbits. A sun with a mane like a lion's smiles at them all. A civic-minded artist has included, low to the ground, an instruction to passersby: *Do not urinate.*

There are children here. The students, presumably. They hold stick brooms and sweep the grounds around the school building. Bent over like that, one hand on knee, the other on the handle of a broom, sweeping dust from dust—the children's posture is that of service. It moves PT Sir. This is what a school ought to teach, he thinks. How come his school doesn't instill such feeling in the students?

When a party assistant arrives, he recognizes PT Sir, thumping him on the back and asking how the school building looks. PT Sir says, "First class!"

"Have you seen inside?" the assistant asks. The two of them walk up to the door and peep in.

There is a vacant room. It looks incomplete, until PT Sir realizes there will be no benches here, no chairs. The children are used to sitting on the ground. Probably they will share one textbook, photocopied to death. After the first wave of donated supplies runs out, the children will write with pencil nubs chewed and sucked.

Still they will come to school.

"And look at my own students," PT Sir shares. "They are fed and clothed and schooled, given every convenience and comfort."

"My son," agrees the assistant, "goes to extra coaching for every subject. English, maths, chemistry, everything. I think, what are they teaching him at school? If they are not teaching him the subjects, are they teaching him manners, loyalty to the country, et cetera, et cetera? No!"

The two men pause when a box of sweets comes around.

"Take my students," says PT Sir. "Will they ever sweep the school grounds? Will they ever paint a beautiful mural like this? Never! Because they"—and here he pauses to chew his sweet—"are trying their level best to flee the country. They work so hard on applications to American universities that they ignore the school exams, failing and crying and pleading—they had SAT I! They had SAT II! What are these nonsense exams? Why will the school allow such brain drain?"

The party man listens intently. When he is done with his sweet, he claps crumbs off his hands, then clasps his hands behind his back like a diligent schoolboy. "The problem, you see," he joins in, "is we teach our children many things, but not national feeling! There is a scarcity of patriotic feeling, don't you think so? In our generation, we knew our schooling was to . . . was to . . ."

"Serve others," offers PT Sir. "Improve the nation."

"Exactly!"

The thought stays with him when he returns to his school. The girls run a simple relay race. They huff and puff, carrying a stick in their hands, and afterward lean on their knees to catch their breath.

They high-five and laugh so loud a teacher from the third floor emerges to give them a stern look.

What is the meaning of such an education? PT Sir thinks as he walks down the lane at the end of the day. Around him, girls suck ice candies and call with orange mouths, "Good afternoon, sir!"

JIVAN

THE NEXT TIME PURNENDU COMES, I TRY TO SEE everything the way he must see it. The guard's pacing, and the stench of sweat which rises off her. The benches around us where visitors and inmates sit, a third person's worth of space between them. The instructions painted on the wall:

Please hand all home-cooked food to prison personnel
Please no body contact
Be respectful and talk at low volume
Any cell phone or camera will be confiscated

"Have you printed the first part of my story?" I demand.

Once more he has placed that useless pen on the bench between us. The guard has seen it, but whatever it is, she does not want to deal with it.

Purnendu smiles. "We have hardly begun! Once we have the full story, my editor will help me—"

"Why do you need some editor?" I charge. Then I try to be polite. "I need this story printed. I am telling it to you in order, arranged nicely, exactly how things happened. Just print it. You have to do it quickly, don't you understand?"

Purnendu looks at me and pats my hand, on the bench. How soft his fingertips. I wish he would keep them there, on the bony back of my hand, where my knuckles sprout hairs.

"It doesn't work like that. We want the public to see the full story, beginning to end, rather than leaking a piece here, a piece there. Do you trust me?"

*

THE MORNING AFTER THE EVICTION, when we woke up in a displeased aunt's house in the neighboring village, my father complained of "a little pain." His neck was held stiff, his whole body turning when he looked this way and that. This new village bordered a site at which garbage was burned. The rot and smoke made us all feel sick. But my father, I could see, was injured, perhaps from a policeman's blow.

My mother, her own bones sore, lay quietly in bed, saying nothing. I took charge, suddenly my parents' parent, and took my father to a doctor who, the aunt told us, was part of a clinic at a district government hospital. There the doctor saw the poor and the illiterate for no more than a flat fee of twenty rupees.

The hospital compound looked like a village in itself. Under the trees, on the porch, every spot of shade was taken by a family. Each family surrounded a patient who lay, moaning or blank-faced, on unfolded leaves of newspaper. My father walked straight past them, looking ahead and nowhere else. Into the hospital building we went, and I filled out a form and paid twenty rupees. Then we sat in a room, under a ceiling fan whose blades were so weighted with cottony dust that they barely moved. My father held a gentle hand to his shoulder, not rubbing it, but seeking to soothe it in some way that was beyond him. Finally, the doctor called us, "Patient party? Where is the patient?"

"He," I began, calling my father by the respectful pronoun, "he has a lot of pain in his shoulder." We scrambled into the tiny chamber, and sat in two chairs, both with woven seats on the verge of tearing from the weight of hundreds of patients over the years. On the wall fluttered a calendar with pictures of pink-cheeked babies. "Please see what happened to his shoulder," I said.

My father looked at the doctor, his eyes glistening with tears he would not release.

"Fell, or what?" said the doctor, looking at us over his spectacles.

"No, they hit him," I said.

Immediately, as the doctor asked, "Who hit him?" my father spoke up.

"Somebody on the road," my father said, with a small smile. "Who knows? It doesn't matter. I am only here for some medicine. I couldn't sleep last night because of the—"

My father cried in pain. The doctor had reached over and was laying cold fingertips on my father's upper back, pressing at various points. My father, whose calves had carried three people at once up slopes in his rickshaw. My father, whose back leaned forward in strength as he pedaled, up and down, up and down, for twenty-five rupees per ride. A tense silence descended on the room.

I grew angry—why wasn't my father telling the doctor the police did it? Catch the police! Put them in jail for hurting him like that! How would he drive the rickshaw again with such pain?

Now I understand his silence. Now I know his reluctance.

The doctor stopped his examination and spoke in an irritated tone. "You could have gone to a general physician and had an X-ray first, why didn't you do that? I can't give you anything except this painkiller when you have come like this, with no test. Maybe the bone here is broken, but maybe not. How can I tell? You are not letting me touch the place, saying, 'Oo aa, I am in pain.' Go get the X-ray first—"

"Yes, yes, sir," my father said, timid. "Can you write it down, please, the X-ray place where I should go—"

"Do you know how to read?" the doctor demanded.

"My daughter knows," said my father. Even in his pain, he looked at me and smiled with pride.

*

WHEN I RETURN TO my cell, it smells like flowers. Americandi is surrounded by five or six others, including Yashwi, who is spraying something from a bottle.

I sneeze.

"Not in your armpit!" Americandi scolds her. "You don't even know *how* to put perfume. Like this," she says, "watch me."

Americandi turns her chin up and tilts the bottle at her neck. Striated with lines, a column wobbly with fat, her neck newly glistens with a patch of scent.

"Like this," she says once more, now holding a delicate wrist upturned. "You have to put it on the places where your blood is beating."

"Then why aren't you putting it on your chest?" someone challenges her.

"I wish we had a party!" Kalkidi moans. "Don't we smell so nice?"

"Smell it," Americandi demands when she sees me. She hands me the bottle. "Pure rose and . . . and . . . !" She thinks for a moment. "Some other things. Doesn't it smell costly? Even Twinkle Khanna wears this perfume."

I wipe my nose with the back of my hand, and sniff the air around me. It smells like roses and chemicals. It smells like a disguise. Beneath it, there is sewage and damp and washed clothes hung to dry. There is indigestion and belching and the odor of feet.

For a moment, I wonder how Americandi has the means to buy expensive perfume. Then, of course, I know.

On the floor, I see a thick new mattress. On top, folded, are a soft blanket and clean sheets. Now I hear the crinkle of paper behind me, and turn to see

Kalkidi holding a bar of Cadbury chocolate. Ameri-candi holds up a dozen more bars.

"For the children!" she says, and a mother looks like she will cry.

Her purchases agitate me. I could have bought a few things for myself. Oils and soaps, some cream biscuits to eat. A better mattress, a sheet with polka dots. I could have given most of it to Ma and Ba. Ba's medicines are not cheap. What have I done?

Late into the night I think about this, regret raising its head like a snake in the bushes. Is one story in a newspaper going to persuade anyone?

LOVELY

ONE MORNING, ON THE WAY TO A BLESSING CERE-
mony in a nearby village, the boys in front of the
tailor's shop are staring, so I am teasing: "You want
to visit my bed, just tell me!"

They are ashamed and giggling at the floor, holding scissors in their hands.

In this life, everybody is knowing how to give me
shame. So I am learning how to reflect shame back
on them also.

At this pre-marriage party, where we are coming
to bless and earn money that way, we are climbing
up to a roof where, under one old towel drying on a
string, there is an old woman, the bride's grandma.
With her knees folded on the ground, she is pumping air into an old harmonium and playing the keys,
which are the color of elephant tusks. The thin gold
bangles on her arms are clinking softly as she is
pumping and playing, pumping and playing. In the
gentle winter sun, in the breeze, I am seeing her as
a young woman, learning to play harmonium. The
morning is softening for me.

Then Arjuni Ma is singing, and I am stepping in the center and loosening my shoulders, pinching a bit of sari in my left hand to lift the hem away from the ground, and with my right hand making stars and suns in the air. Arjuni Ma is singing an old romantic classic. I am turning this way and that way, and with my turns my sari is flowing like a stream, catching the light. I am using my eyes to match the expressions in the song, I am really "emoting," as Mr. Debnath would say. Now my eyes are loving, now they are seducing, now they are looking shyly at the ground, as if Azad is sitting right here too among the women. Since I was telling him to marry a woman, he is not coming to see me even one time. What a mistake! I was thinking I would be feeling noble, but no, I am only feeling sad.

Though this is a private ceremony, some donkey villagers are standing in the doorway, spilling down the stairs, laughing and pointing, taking pictures of me with their mobile phones. What can I be doing? This is my job, to perform.

The bride-to-be is shyly sitting on the ground, looking at the dancing. She is wrapped in a starched yellow sari, and eating peeled cucumber dipped in pink salt.

When I am getting tired of dancing, and sweat is starting to pour down my back, I am bending and taking the bride's chin in my hands, saying, "God keep this beautiful girl in rice and gold."

Finally the mother of the bride, who is standing in the doorway, is seeing me admiring the girl's looks, and she is complaining, "This girl is getting so dark! You tell her, please. She is always riding her bicycle in the hot sun, no umbrella, no nothing."

So I am giving the bride a sideways look and saying, "Why, child? Now you put some yogurt and lemon on that face! Look at me, dark and ugly, do you think anybody wants to marry me?"

"Yes!" the girl's mother is saying. "Are you listening? Listen to her. She is telling you these things from experience. It is for your own good."

So this is how my job is. You can be making fun of me, but tell me, can you be doing this job?

PT SIR

"MORE ANTI-NATIONAL STATEMENTS HAVE BEEN UN-covered," shouts a reporter standing at the Kolabagan railway station, "after the *Your News, Your Views* team studied Jivan's Facebook page. She posted seditious statements, no doubt testing whether—"

PT Sir's wife picks up the remote and lowers the volume.

"This student of yours!" she complains. "This case will go on forever. You went to the police, you did your part. When did we last do something fun?"

So, after dinner, PT Sir and his wife leave the house and walk to the local video rental shop, a one-room operation called Dinesh Electronics. Inside, before shelves of lightbulbs and wires, the owner sits viewing his own stock, surreptitiously stored on tiny USB sticks, no bigger than half a thumb. These recordings of the newest movies he rents out.

"Try this one, sister," he suggests to PT Sir's wife. "*Something Happens in My Heart When I See Her*! In demand this week, I just got it back from a customer.

New actress in it, Rani Sarawagi. And filmed fully in Switzerland!"

PT Sir's wife accepts the USB stick and tucks it in her purse. Outside, the air smells of fried food. A vendor dips lentil balls in a dark wok filled with oil, and sells paper bowls full, alongside a cilantro and green chili chutney. Next to him, a shoe repairman works under the thin light of a bulb, gluing a separated sole.

The sidewalk is cracked and uneven, so PT Sir and his wife keep to the edge of the road, near the dry gutter, as they walk. Headlights of cars approach and swerve by. Often, there is no space to walk side by side.

*

WHEN THE END CREDITS roll across the TV screen, PT Sir shares his big news of the day.

"Oh, I almost forgot!" he feigns.

His wife looks at him, smiling from the romantic closing of the film, where the hero and the heroine found their way to each other and embraced on an Alpine meadow.

"I got a lunch invitation," PT Sir says. "Bimala Pal invited me to her house."

He speaks calmly. But he is aware that his heart is beating a little fast. The sleep has fled his eyes.

"Bimala Pal?" says his wife, surprised. "Lunch at her *house*? Why, what does she want?"

PT Sir braces himself. His wife will, no doubt, caution him against going. So far, she has said nothing about the school inauguration, for which he took a half day off work, but—

She laughs. "Look at you," she says. "First she comes to your school, now this. Maybe she really likes you!"

PT Sir smiles, relieved.

"Remember to take a box of nice sweets," she tells him, "not those cheap sweets you eat."

JIVAN

IN THE MIDDLE OF TV HOUR, WHEN THE ROOM IS louder with our commentary than television, Uma madam appears, showily eating a pear.

"You." She points at me with the bitten pear. "Somebody to see you."

I jump up. My back seizes, a shock traveling up and down my spine. Clutching a hand to it, I make my way to the visiting room, where the lawyer Gobind waits.

"Where did you go?" I demand. "Every time I try to call you, I stand in line for half an hour, pay so much money to call, and then your assistant picks up—"

He holds both hands up. "I have seventy-four cases on my desk," he says. "I can't sit around waiting for your call. Anyway, I am doing the work, aren't I? I contacted the leader of your Lovely's hijra group. Her name is Arjuni. Do you know her?"

I shake my head.

"She told me that Lovely left," he says.

"What?"

"She said that Lovely went to her native village—"

"Where is that?"

"In the north. She doesn't know exactly."

I look at him for a long while. He coughs into a fist, and says, "Want to tell me anything?"

"You think I'm lying?" I say. "That leader is lying. *You* are lying, for all I know! Did you even look for Lovely, or do you think she is an imaginary character I have made up?"

I lower my voice. "I will tell my mother to go find Lovely. I am sure she is here. She never mentioned any village to me. She will come testify if I ask her. She will tell them that I was teaching her, that the parcel I was carrying was books for her."

"Try," sighs Gobind.

INTERLUDE

GOBIND VISITS A SPIRITUAL GURU

BY FRIDAY AT LUNCHTIME, MY OFFICE IRRITATES ME. There is no painless way to arrange my belly before my desk. The termite tracks on the wall seem to grow every time I look away. My assistant treats his hoarse cough by smoking cigarettes with greater devotion. When the phone rings, it is my daughter's school saying my daughter has been suspended for breaking a fellow student's spectacles. I call her mother. Her mother will pick her up. I have too much work.

Days like this, only one thing helps. I visit my guru. My guru, my spiritual leader, is in her seventies, and lives on the ground floor of a house where the door is always open. Her living room has idols of gods on all surfaces. It smells of morning flowers. She does not eat meat, does not leave her house, does not watch TV. Once, I saw an iPad on her lap, but she put it away. She meditates. Her only bad habit is, she feeds stray dogs.

"I thought you would come today, child," she says,

looking up from petting a tan stray. The dog barks. I hold my arms up as the dog jumps on my knees. I don't like dogs. My guru calls the dog away, and instantly it settles at her feet and looks at me.

"I saw some clouds in your life," my guru says. "But clouds pass."

A glass of water appears in front of me, and I tell her everything. I even tell her what I was not planning to reveal. My wife is upset with me. She thinks I spend too much money on my guru's recommendations—an onyx ring one day, a smoky quartz another day. But a garnet worn on the left pinky helped me win my first case. I am sure of it. A white coral, which is in fact red, helped me avoid a deadly accident on my regular route home, when a tree fell on top of a taxi in front of me. I have worn a green tourmaline close to my chest, I have worn a moonstone. The day I began wearing a golden citrine, a frightening medical test came back benign. Don't tell me there's nothing here. The world is made up of negativity, problems, hassles—trust me, a lawyer knows—and gemstones bring good energy.

I have sixty to eighty cases at any time. A big case like Jivan's means nothing but more misery— a dozen press people hounding me at all hours, pressure from all political parties, daily communication with police chiefs trying to hide their inept investigations. No matter the result, there will be plenty of people upset with me. It is trouble. The sooner it ends, the better for me.

"Will it end soon?" I ask. "It's too much."

My guru tells me yes, it will, but—she pauses.

"Your role," she says with a gentle smile, "will be bigger than you can see at the moment."

"In a good way?" I ask.

"In a good way," she says. "When paths show themselves, don't be afraid to follow them."

And I feel lifted on a wave and placed on a shore. I get up. I should call my wife, I think. Check how my daughter is handling her suspension. I need to get back to my office before the assistant turns it into an ashtray. On the road I will eat an egg roll.

"Your wife may not support my suggestion," my guru says, "but I am getting a strong feeling that one thing will be especially valuable for you during this time. For your right index finger"—and here she holds up the finger she means—"an amethyst."

JIVAN

PURNENDU HAS BROUGHT ME A STRING OF SHAMPOO sachets, clothesline clips, and elastic hair bands. I hold the gifts in my lap. They are currency.

"Thanks," I say to him in English, so that he knows, even while he gives me products with which I will clean myself and groom myself, that I can be his equal.

*

WE RESETTLED IN GOVERNMENT housing in a town, fifty kilometers away from our village, with nothing in it but buildings whose walls were plump with damp, whose sewage flowed in open gutters, whose taps coughed rusty water. But it was my first and only time living in an apartment building, and I was proud of my residence.

I heard the neighbor boy, fellow evicted, stomp down the stairs every evening. I watched, from the window, as he emerged into the lane, where a cohort gathered to play cricket. A plank of plywood served as a bat, and the fielders chased a hollow plastic ball.

They were my age. My limbs itched to play with them, to scream and run and skid on the small pebbles of the street, now that my known fields were gone. My mother said no.

I was a girl. I stayed home to watch my father, while my mother left at dawn and returned in the evening, seeking daily labor. A few days she was employed on construction projects, but after that, the jobs ran out.

Then my mother cooked, hidden in the kitchen. An atmosphere of smoke and chili about her deterred conversation.

One night, I heard her and my father.

"Where is the work?" my mother said. "Everybody here is resettled like us. Who will hire me?"

"Wait a few days," said my father. "I will take a loan to buy a new rickshaw."

"Another rickshaw," my mother mocked. "Who will ride your rickshaw in this cursed town?"

I was ashamed to hear everything. I was ashamed to see my mother sinking into this gray mood.

I crept up on her one day as she was cooking.

"Bhow!" I said behind her. She jumped and smacked at my legs, but I escaped. From the doorway I said, in a monster's deep voice, "Ow mow khow! I smell some human chow!"

I crept closer, allowing my mother to take another swipe at my legs, to trap me this time, but she did not try.

*

SO THAT IS HOW I grew up, you see, Purnendu. When Ba's turn in the X-ray came, I took him. We took a bus which sped down the highway, horn blasting, and brought us to an air-conditioned clinic. I gave a look to a woman until she moved her bag, so that Ba could take the chair. The woman's arms were white and plump. Diamonds sparkled on her fingers. Her feet were wrapped in the crisscrossing strings of a leather sandal, and her toenails were painted pink. They looked like lozenges. She looked at us. I slid one cracked and soiled foot behind the other.

In a dark room, a technician positioned Ba against a cold glass plate, then disappeared. Ba flinched.

"Stand still!" scolded the technician, from a chamber we could not see. "Stand straight!"

But the X-ray man could not make the picture. He came out, irritated.

"What's the matter?" he said.

Ba rubbed his bare skin, chilled. Still he smiled as a way of asking forgiveness. "It's cold—"

"The plate is *supposed* to be cold!" said the X-ray man. "You have to stand firm, touching it, that's what I *told* you. I can't do my work with these unschooled people—"

Afterward I held the large envelope in my hand, within it a ghostly image of Ba's back and shoulders. I carried it home, like a parent carrying their child's schoolbag, the weight too heavy for the young one to bear.

At home, I began to show Ma the scan, but she shouted, "Put it back, put it back! You can't look at these things without a special light, or it will be ruined. Fool child."

Was that right? I did what she said.

"X-ray today, then something else tomorrow," said my mother. "Wait and see, that doctor will keep you running around. That's what doctors do. They get paid to make you do tests and buy medicines, don't you know that? Where will we get the money?"

My father sat on the bed and, keeping his neck stiff, swung his legs up. He listened to my mother.

But I knew something was wrong. If I did nothing, Ba would suffer. At least, we had to show the X-ray plates to the doctor.

A rickshaw-driver friend of Ba's gave us his service one morning, rolling gently over the potholes that led out of the block of apartment buildings and on to the main road. Ba's eyes filled with water. He arrived at the hospital, defeated by the ride.

"Hmm," said the doctor, after we had waited for three hours, and Ba had nearly fallen and broken one more bone while going to the slippery toilet. "The bone *is* broken, do you see here?"

He pointed a pen at the ghostly image.

"But there is a more serious problem," he continued. "This disk has been affected, and that is serious. He needs absolute bed rest, otherwise there will be a chance of paralysis. And I see he is in pain, so he needs stronger medicines. Take this twice a day, with food."

"I *said* he was in pain," I complained, leaning forward in my chair. "He has been in pain since we first came to see you."

"Listen, why are you being so agitated?" The doctor put down his pen and glared at me. "For some people an ant's bite is also serious pain."

Then he continued writing in his prescription book. In a penholder, a pen printed with the name of a pharmaceutical company shined.

"And what about the rickshaw, doctor shaheb?" my father asked. "I have to go back to work soon."

"Work?" said the doctor. "Be patient, mister. It's enough that you walked in here on your own. You can't drive a rickshaw anytime soon."

*

AFTER WEEKS OF RUNNING to a municipal tube well early every morning and carrying water up five flights of stairs, Ma and I began going to the water board office, complaining about the rust-colored water spat out by the taps.

At the water office, a man with a ring of hair surrounding a bald head waved us away—he had begun to recognize us—as soon as we approached.

"Later, come later," he said. "I told you I can't do anything about the water in two–three days."

"Sir, we came seven–ten days ago."

"Is that so?" he said. "Now you know my schedule better than me?"

"We still don't have clean water, sir," said my mother, "and they said that by July—"

"Who said?" charged the man, pausing in the

chewing of gum. "*Who* said such things? July, August, am I in charge of carrying the water from here to your house?"

Ma said nothing, and I felt like a small child next to her, though I was as much a grown-up as anybody in that office.

It was too much. "Sir, actually," I said, "you told us last time that the water supply would be fixed soon. My father is sick. He can't climb down five flights of stairs to the municipal tap for his baths." My cheeks were hot. My voice was hoarse. "Please do something, sir."

The man stared at me, eyes bulging, before picking up a phone.

"Yes, good morning," he said softly into the phone, a polite professional. "What happened to the work order for the water pipes . . ." He went on in this way, while we stood and looked at him. I was delighted, though the only expression I could wear was one of pleading.

Three days later, when the taps in our building deposited clean water into our buckets, my mother told everyone it was all my doing.

"Jivan spoke to the water supply man," she recounted to the neighbors. "Oh, you should have seen her!"

Later, in the quiet of the kitchen after we had eaten, she said to me, "The system doesn't always work for us. But you see that, now and then, you can make good things happen for yourself."

And I thought, only *now and then*? I thought I would have a better life than that.

PT SIR

A POLITICIAN'S HOUSE IS MARKED BY AN ATMOSPHERE like a fair at all times. Feet from the door, reporters wait idly, smoking cigarettes and tossing them in the gutter. Clerks and lackeys keep an eye on those coming and going, occasionally stopping to chat with this or that person. Citizens with grievances arrive, holding folders. Less frequently arrive packages, sometimes a bouquet or a gift basket of dried fruit. Down the road, policemen assigned to the politician wait inside a vehicle. They sit, rifles strapped to their backs, the doors open for air.

On the porch, where PT Sir takes off his shoes, grateful for his clean socks, an assistant asks him: "You have an appointment?"

"No, I mean," says PT Sir, "I got a lunch invitation, so—"

"Oh," says the assistant, opening the door. "You are the teacher."

The house is ordinary. Apart from a few framed photographs of parents and grandparents, garlanded by fragrant white flowers, the walls are bare. Two sofas, with rather regal upholstery, face each other, and beyond them stands a dining table with six chairs. The floor is laid with flecked tiles, as in any middle-class home. Some of the tiles are cracked.

PT Sir stands on this cold floor in socked feet, unsure of himself, until Bimala Pal emerges from an inner office. She invites him to sit at the dining table, whose plywood surface is covered by a plastic cloth which mimics lace. Dishes appear from the kitchen. The food is humble—rice, dal, and fried eggplant, followed by rui fish curry. When, PT Sir wonders, will Bimala Pal tell him why he has been invited? She seems unconcerned.

"Just yesterday I was in Bankura district," says Bimala Pal, "and you know what is happening there? The midday meal funds for schools are disappearing into the pockets of school administrators. Those children are getting rice full of stones, lentils cooked in a tiny bit of oil. I said . . ." The story ends with a student's grandmother crying with gratitude in Bimala Pal's embrace.

It is when their plates are almost clean that Bimala Pal says, "You must be thinking why I have asked to see you today."

PT Sir looks at her, and her plate, where she has made a pile of fish bones, curved like miniature swords.

"You see, I have a small hassle on my hands," she says. "I was thinking, maybe an educated man like yourself can help us with it."

PT Sir sees, through the open door, a dark figure

in the sun, holding a baby. A clerk comes by and says, "Madam, the society of mothers who—"

"Coming, coming," says Bimala Pal.

"The engineers are also waiting—"

Bimala Pal nods, and the clerk retreats.

There isn't much time.

"I will be honored to help you in any way," PT Sir finds himself saying. "Tell me, what can I do?"

*

SO IT IS THAT, a few weeks later, PT Sir finds himself at the courthouse. The grand British-era building has received a new coat of brick-red paint. Surrounding the building is a large garden planted with rows of hibiscus and marigold. Even at the early morning hour, the grounds have an air of harried activity. Lawyers in black robes cross the yard. PT Sir lets himself be passed. Under a row of oak trees, typists sit before typewriters, beside them stacks of legal paper. Next to them, tea-samosa sellers, resting kettles and cups on the ground, engage in a brisk trade.

No one pays any attention to PT Sir, so nobody notices that he is sweating excessively, armpit patches spreading under the blazer he has worn. His left thumb twitches, a tremor that he has never had before. He hides the hand in his pocket.

Up he goes into the old courthouse, then down a long balcony, off which he can see, through doors left ajar, a library with ceiling fans turning at the top. He walks by warrens of lawyers' offices, stuffed with leaning towers of folders. PT Sir retrieves a handkerchief from his trousers' pocket and mops his damp forehead. Before courtroom A6, he taps a guard at a door, clears his throat, and says, "I am a witness."

Then he sits on a hard wooden bench, watching in anxiety as three other cases are swiftly brought before the judge and resolved.

Half an hour later, when PT Sir is called to the front of the courtroom, his throat is parched, and while his left thumb has stopped twitching, his right eyelid has taken up the tendency. He walks slowly, trying to project calm. He stands in a witness box, and a clerk warns him not to lean on the railing. It wobbles.

Before him appears a lawyer wearing a wrinkled robe and summer sandals with chapped edges. PT Sir looks at those feet, then at the room of dozing men awaiting their own hearings.

Now Bimala Pal seems very far away, her influence no more than a gentle memory.

PT Sir wonders in a panic if he can get out of this.

Is there a way? Maybe he can fake a heart attack.

The lawyer asks him: *"Habyusinthisparson?"*

"Hmm?" says PT Sir. He coughs, and clears his throat.

He has spoken. Can he fake a heart attack now?

The lawyer says it again, and this time PT Sir understands what he is saying: "Have you seen this person?"

The lawyer indicates a man seated at a table in front. The man wears an oversize blue shirt with short sleeves that fall to his blackened elbows. Through his half-open mouth, PT Sir can see that his teeth are stained red.

PT Sir knows none of these men, not the man with the stained teeth, nor the lawyer, but his job, per Bimala Pal's assistant's instructions, is to say: Yes, he has come across that man. He saw that man fleeing after a hardware store near his school was robbed.

PT Sir has never seen this man before, of course, but he knows—he has been told—that this is a man who has robbed and stolen for a living, but never been caught. There has never been evidence, though his neighbors and friends all know the truth. It is true that he also belongs to the wrong religion, the minority religion that encourages the eating of beef, but that is a peripheral matter, according to Bimala Pal's assistant. The main issue is, a robber has to be stopped. What decent man would object to participating in the execution of justice?

Now PT Sir has to speak, or else faint. He must speak, or else surrender all hope of moving up in life by Bimala Pal's grace.

So, with his cool, teacher's diction, his nicely combed hair, his button-down shirt and black blazer, never mind the damp armpits, he stands before that filthy-faced, rotten-toothed criminal, and says, "Him, yes, that man, I saw him there. He was running in a direction away from the hardware store."

Then, with an exchange between the lawyer and the judge that PT Sir does not follow, the matter is over. The criminal is taken away by a policeman to pay a hefty fine, or else go to jail. It is clear that he does not have the means to pay a fine. When he walks past PT Sir, the man looks at him closely, squinting as if he is missing his spectacles. PT Sir turns away. The clerk calls the case number for the next case; the lawyer vanishes; a different set of people approach the bench.

PT Sir strolls casually out of the courtroom, unbuttoning his blazer. His neck prickles as he anticipates how the lawyer will reappear and challenge him. He waits for the judge to call him into chambers and demand to know who he really is. As he passes by guards patrolling the courthouse grounds, he expects an arm to shoot out and bar his way.

But, in a moment, he is on the street, where nothing more distressing happens than this: A pigeon pecking at the ground takes flight and flaps away from him, its wings nearly brushing his face.

*

IN THE MONTHS FOLLOWING, when Bimala Pal's assistant calls PT Sir and gives him a case, he prepares by purchasing a tube of antiperspirant and applying the white gel in his armpits. He carries a bottle of water and sips from it. He goes to sleep early the night before. Perhaps it is these measures, but PT Sir finds, by his fourth time at the courthouse, that there is little that agitates him.

At the doors to the courtroom, the guard greets PT Sir familiarly.

"All well?" he says.

"All well," says PT Sir. "Has my case started yet?"

"Going a bit late today," the guard says. "Not to worry. You go sit in the canteen, I'll send someone to call you."

For the first time, as he wanders down the familiar corridor, past the law library and to the canteen, PT Sir wonders if the guard is paid by the party too. For that matter, how about the courtroom clerks, and the judges, and the lawyers? Not one of them has ever said: "This man is really something! Everywhere there is a robbery, a domestic problem, a fight between neighbors, this man happens to be walking by! Is he Batman or what?"

But now is not the time to think about such things.

An hour and a chicken cutlet later, PT Sir takes the stand, opposite a man in a check-patterned lungi, knotted below a thin, hard belly.

PT Sir says, "This is the man I saw on the road. He was eve-teasing a lady. Making some disgusting gestures. Don't ask me to repeat them." He puts his teeth on his tongue in a gesture of shame and shakes his head. "God knows what would have happened to the lady if I wasn't going that way."

The accused looks bewildered. He opens his mouth to speak and is reminded by the judge to be quiet.

*

THIS IS HOW BIMALA PAL explained it to him, and this is how he explains it to his wife. All these cases are instances in which the police are one hundred and ten percent sure that the accused is guilty. They don't have that much evidence, is all. But the accused are known in their neighborhoods. They have reputations. Should these dangerous men return to the streets on a technicality? Much better to fill the gap with a witness and make sure the guilty party lands in jail.

PT Sir cannot disagree. It is true that there is a lot about life that the law misses. And it doesn't hurt that each assignment comes with a "gift," delivered to him every month by an assistant, perhaps the assistant's assistant, who drives to the house on a noisy motorcycle and offers a pristine white envelope.

LOVELY

TODAY, WHEN MR. DEBNATH IS GIVING US A SCENE
where we are having to express tears, many of us are
looking concerned.

"I have heard," Rumeli is saying, "that on real sets
they are using some burning eye drops—"

"Burning eye drops!" Mr. Debnath's voice is boom-
ing. He is seeing red.

"If you want to be a C-level actor you can use all
those cheap things!" he is saying. "Real actors cry
from the heart. Real actors are reaching into their
own selves, and not imagining a false sad moment,
but returning to a true sad moment in their own life.
That is how you are crying real tears in a made-up
scene."

We are all nodding seriously then. Mr. Debnath is
saying such deep things.

*

UNTIL I WAS THIRTEEN–FOURTEEN years old, I was
living with my parents, who were both working in the

local post office, and my grandparents, two uncles, their wives and children, all of us stuffed in a four-room apartment with a small balcony where we were sprinkling puffed rice for sparrows to eat. We were neither rich, neither poor. Once a month we were going to the movie theater after eating rice and egg at home. The popcorn counter was not existing for people like us.

In the outside world, I was wearing boy's shorts and a boy's haircut, and playing cricket. But secretly, at home, I was trying lipstick. I was wearing my mother's saris once, twice, thrice. The fourth time my uncles were persuading my father to kick me out of the house. "What dignity will we have with this unnatural boy in the household?" they were shouting. "Our children are normal, think about them!"

My cousins were hiding in a bedroom, peeping out at me with big eyes.

My mother was fighting to keep me at home. She was saying I could be going to a special school! I could be seeing a doctor! But how long can a mother be fighting against the laws of society? So I was leaving.

In my heart I am knowing that my grieving mother must have been looking for me for years. Maybe she is still searching for me. I am not thinking about her anymore.

When I was first finding my way to the hijra house, I was learning singing and dancing, the art of charming strangers and persuading them. In classes run by an NGO, I was continuing my studies of Bengali and arithmetic, until their funding ended. So I was never learning a lot from books. When I was a child, I was being taught that school was the most important thing in the world—my exams and my marks would make me successful! These days, I am seeing that's not true. Was Gandhiji spending his time sitting on top of a book? Was Rakhee, the greatest film star in history, spending her time saying no, please, cannot make films due to I am having to study a book? No. Me, I am learning from life.

*

LOVELY IS MY HIJRA NAME, which I was selecting at my eighteenth birthday ceremony. That was the ceremony where I was becoming a real woman. Arjuni Ma was taking me into her own bedroom and standing me in front of a tall mirror. She was giving me a golden blouse and a black petticoat to wear, and then she was wrapping a red sari around my hips. Her old knuckles and wrinkled skin were touching me with so much love. I was looking at myself in the mirror, making myself to be thinking of some jokes so that I was not crying. Finally I was knowing what it was feeling like, to be all the women I was seeing every day—on the train, holding children's hands, cooking with ginger-garlic. They were all doing this one thing before going out of the house, putting nine yards of fabric on their bodies. When Arjuni Ma was kneeling in front of me, separating the pleats, I was true to god giving up and sobbing.

That whole night I was dancing with my sisters. The Bollywood classics on the stereo were making me feel like a star, like my body was silk and gold.

Everybody's eyes were watching me, full of admiration. Many of the sisters were having, how to say, eighty percent energy, twenty percent talent. But for me, it was different. I was turning round and round, and seeing the pink balloons and golden streamers like a film-set decoration. Even the dim tubelight of the room was looking to me like a spotlight.

Only one thing was making me sad. I am still not liking to think about it, but Mr. Debnath has given this assignment, so. I was knowing that even the sisters who were smiling sweetly were secretly complaining to each other: "Can you imagine, Lovely has not even had the cutting-cutting operation! But Arjuni Ma is giving her the ceremony anyway, what luck!"

*

A LONG TIME AGO, before my ceremony, my closest sister in the hijra house was Ragini. When Ragini was turning eighteen, she was going with Arjuni Ma to a dentist's chamber for her operation. She was asking me to come also, and I was saying, yes, of course, so that after the operation we could be having ice candy!

The dentist's chamber was having a sign saying *Closed*, but when Arjuni Ma was knocking, a man who was talking on his Nokia phone was opening the door. Inside, the room was partitioned by a curtain which was only going halfway to the floor. Behind it there was a small space with stacks of medicine samples on the floor, and a few calendars which were also never put up. On the topmost calendar there was a photo of a foreign baby with such deep dimples. I was almost smiling to see that baby, but the smell of the room, like a damp towel, was bringing me back. Above us I was seeing black patches of mold on the ceiling, and a narrow bed which was covered with canvas sheeting, like a raincoat. When Arjuni Ma was giving her permission, Ragini was taking off her pants and lying down on this bed.

Arjuni Ma was telling me to stand above Ragini's head and be holding her hands. Ragini was so brave. In my eyes that day, Ragini was a heroine. When the doctor was entering the room, his face was already covered with a mask, so I was never knowing if this was the man on the phone or a different man. Arjuni Ma was telling Ragini to begin her chanting, and Ragini was repeating the name of the goddess over and over. Chanting the name was supposed to make the ceremony blessed by god, and also keep the pain away.

At this point I was feeling a bit scared. I was holding Ragini's hand tighter and I was whispering: "From tomorrow all the Romeos will be falling for you."

Ragini was smiling with her dark gums.

The dentist was saying, mumbling mumbling, that he was having no anesthetic that day. How I don't know, but I was having a gut feeling that he was lying. My gut was telling me that he was feeling nervous about using anesthetics, even when he was having them in stock. But without anesthetics Ragini was facing an impossible amount of pain. I was asking the doctor, "Why don't you give her a little bit of anesthetic, sir, or some numbing medicine?"

At that he was getting irritated. "You are doing the operation or me?"

I was having nothing to say then.

Ragini was interrupting, "No problem, what is some pain? Some painkiller I will take after the operation." She was looking at me, like *don't make the doctor angry*. She was eager to do the operation. So I was keeping my mouth shut.

I was keeping my eyes shut too. Just the sight of the blade was too much, leave alone the blood. With eyes closed I was hearing the sounds—Arjuni Ma breathing sharply, some liquid squirting, something metal hitting the side of the table. When I was opening my eyes, so much bright red blood was in between Ragini's legs, I was thinking that Ragini was now a full woman. She was even getting a period.

Then I was thinking, Ragini was dead.

Then, Ragini was not dead. She was a ghost. She was not screaming, not crying. Her head was lolling from right to left, like her skull was loose on her neck, and she was shivering like she was having 104 degrees fever. Her hands in my hands were blocks of ice. I was letting them go and crying, "Arjuni Ma, see what Ragini is doing! She is acting strange!"

Arjuni Ma was watching the doctor like an eagle.

At last, with the help of many rags and one no-question-asking taxi driver, we were cleaning up Ragini's wound and transporting her back to the house. For three–four days she was having high fever, and we were piling more sheets on her to sweat out the temperature. Finally, one day, Ragini was sitting up, accepting the sugar water I was bringing her. She was taking one sip and smiling. I was giving all my thanks to the goddess that day. I was believing in miracles. When Ragini was starting to spend the evenings sitting with us in front of the TV, dancing with her hands when her favorite songs were playing, I was smiling and smiling. I was holding her hand and never letting her go.

Then, one morning, she was not waking up.

"Ragini!" we were calling, "Ragini, wake up!"

I was splashing water on her face. I was pinching her toes. Somebody was putting an old shoe in front of her nose, in case the smell of leather was helping.

But Arjuni Ma was seeing, and I was seeing also, that Ragini was gone very far from us. Her eyes were still, her lips were cracking, her skin was bloodless. Ragini was dead.

From what was she dead? Nobody was knowing, because all of us, and even Arjuni Ma, were afraid of going to real doctors. But I was knowing, oh I was knowing for sure, one hundred percent, it was the dentist. Maybe his blade was having rust on it, or maybe his hands were not clean. Maybe, without anesthetic, the pain was storing and storing in Ragini's body until she was not being able to take it. Like that, Ragini's life was ending.

So I was sure I was never wanting the operation. I was wanting to stay a half-half my whole life.

*

THAT IS THE PAIN I am recalling in my acting class today, and that is the pain I am carrying with me when I am going home and seeing a woman squatting outside my door. Her head is down, and her hair is silver. Hearing my footsteps, she is standing up, and immediately I am seeing the resemblance: It is Jivan's mother.

Inside, she is sitting on my mattress, because there is nowhere else to sit. With her legs folded, her glistening eyes, her small hands, she is looking like a child. Then she is asking me a question that no mother should be having to ask.

"Mother," I am saying to her afterward, "I am knowing what it is like to lose a loved one. And poor Jivan is also lost, at this moment. But the good thing is that she will be coming back."

Jivan's mother is holding her tea glass in her hand and looking at me, waiting for my lecture to get to the point. So I am saying it clearly.

"I will testify," I am saying. "Don't worry one bit. I will go to the court, I will tell them the truth, that Jivan is one kindhearted child teaching the poors, like myself! She was just a soul doing good for the uglies, like myself! I was having in mind that I would be saying all this when the police were coming, but they were not coming only. And I was not having the courage, mother, to walk into a police station myself."

Now Jivan's mother is crying, and a tear is falling down my own cheek. I am closing my eyes, and Ragini is beside me. This time, Ragini is the one holding my hand through the pain. I am opening my eyes and seeing that it is in fact Jivan's mother who is holding my hand, her tears falling on my palms.

"Jivan was telling me once that you are good at blessing babies and brides," she is saying. "Today, you have given this mother the biggest blessing."

True to god I am crying even more.

JIVAN

AMERICANDI UNWRAPS A PACKAGE OF COSTUME JEW-
elry. I listen to the tinkle on her wrist of two glass
bangles. When speaking with me, she gestures excessively to watch the fall and slide of the new bangles.
Their movement delights her.

I soothe myself with daydreams of Lovely in the
courtroom. Imagine when she comes to my trial and
says, in that bold voice of hers, that the package all
these fools keep talking about was a package full of
old books. My dry lips smile to think of it. Even if they
don't believe me, how can anybody refuse to believe
Lovely?

*

WHEN PURNENDU COMES, I tell him nothing about
Lovely. I don't want to jinx it. But I am happy, so I tell
him about an Eid festival, when the lane before our
apartment building lit up green with bulbs strung in
the trees. I wore a new dress and matching bangles
borrowed from my mother, and looked out the window with nowhere, really, to go. A wealthy man, a

landlord who was making lots of money from this government resettlement program, had ordered a whole goat slaughtered, and it was cooked into biryani. The scent rose up to our window. Late at night, due to the goodness of his heart, we ate. We ate with the whole neighborhood, off Styrofoam plates which we tried to wash and keep.

After dinner, I eyed the vendors who had arrived, anticipating a festive marketplace, with trays of sweets and toys. A few boys bought the cheapest toy—tops— and spun them on the road. Other boys boldly asked for samples of cotton candy and then ran away, until the vendor stopped giving out any.

*

THAT WAS OUR LAST month in that town. When a house became available in the big city, my mother moved us, hauling sacks on the train, where a few people shoved us and grumbled about our belongings. Ba stood beside us, holding himself up by his grip on the seat backs, insisting he could.

*

HOW BIG WAS THE big city! I had never seen a place like this, a tide of people rushing and receding at the railway station, announcements and bell tones over the speakers, and in the middle of it all a man selling newspapers. Somebody stepped on my foot, or his suitcase did.

"Standing in the middle of the road," a voice grumbled, and I jumped to the side.

Men were pushing wheeled carts bearing cold bins of fish, trailing a scent of ice. Other men were hauling sacks of cauliflower on their backs.

"Chai gorom!" cried a vendor. "Hot chai!" He carried a tower of washed glasses and a kettle of tea. I wanted tea, and a bakery biscuit. My stomach gurgled.

I followed my mother and father closely, and eventually the noise of the station opened up onto the impossible scene of a paved road, wide as a river, on which crawled cars of all colors. They beeped and honked. Their drivers leaned out of windows and shouted.

We climbed into a bus that was starting its route, a minibus painted maroon and yellow, with *How-rah to Jadavpur* written in beautiful letters on the side. I read it slowly. When Ba pulled himself up the high steps, straining with his arms, the conductor shouted, "What is this, why have you brought a patient on my bus? If he falls, then who will take the responsibility?"

Ba seated himself in silence, his back stiff, his neck turned to the window.

The conductor thumped the side of the bus, and off it flew, lurching and jolting. Ba refused to make a sound, though I knew he was in pain. The conductor, braced in the doorway, cast a suspicious eye on me.

But I was excited. I was thrilled. I walked down the aisle, uneven planks of wood under my bare feet, and watched the men seated by the window, breeze cooling their bald heads, tubes of newspaper rolled up in their laps. Their shirts were clean and pressed, as if they had never been worn before. I didn't know I was staring until one man said, "What is your name?"

He thought I was a child.

"First time in the city?" he said.

My mother, turning around to look at who he was, said yes, and I said nothing. His city accent intimidated me. In the time that it took me to comprehend his words, he said something new.

"I came here from Bolpur," he continued—a town two hundred kilometers away—"three–four years ago. You're coming from somewhere like that, aren't you? I can't imagine going back to a small place. You will like it here."

I couldn't stop thinking that I wanted to be like him. Clean shirt, shined shoes, a smart way of speaking. I hoped the city would make me rich, like him. He wasn't rich, of course. Later I learned that what he was, was called middle class.

*

I REALIZED HOW FAR we were from being middle class when I saw our house. It was deep in the Kolabagan slum, and though Ma had heard through her networks that it was a house made of brick, that turned out to be half-true.

Ma shouted, "This is the house? *This house?*" as we stood in front of its tarp and tin. "Let me call that fool broker right away," she fumed.

Ba smiled helplessly at the neighbors who were peeping, or else boldly standing in doorways with hands on their hips.

"I'm going to lie down," he said in the end, when he couldn't bear something—the shouting, his broken back—anymore.

*

OVER THE MONTHS, it became Ma's practice to go to the cheap, and illegal, market which sprang up by the railway lines in the middle of the night. There she bought loaves of bread, beets, potatoes, and tiny fish, with which she cooked breakfast. These meals she sold in front of our house at dawn. Through heavy sleep, I heard the swish of her sandals and the clink of ladle against pot. If I opened my eyes, I saw customers standing illuminated in the battery-powered flashlight which stood upright on the ground. The customers, our new neighbors, paid ten rupees for some bread and curry with which they could fill their bellies and begin their day's work.

But my mother had to stop when the rains came, beating on roofs, muddy water rising from the wheels of passing rickshaws churning waves that soaked the stove and licked at our high mattress. I took a bucket, its handle cracked so that I had to hold it by the bottom, and tipped the water out on the street, where it joined a stream in which seedpods and the brown shells of cockroaches floated.

By then, Ba's condition was worse. He lay in bed, his shape barely human. There, the head. A foot slipped outside the sheet. An arm raised to show his pleasure at seeing me. While he slept, Ma cooked and cleaned, refusing to speak her worry. But I knew what it was. His medicines cost money, and the monsoon wouldn't let her run her breakfast business. What would we do?

PT SIR

ON THE LAST MORNING OF THE SUMMER HOLIDAY, PT Sir feels the mattress shift under him as his wife wakes. Up she sits, swinging her legs to the ground, yawning noisily, a whiff of her morning breath reaching him. He does not mind. He does not even think about it. He falls back into the delicious sleep of ten more minutes. Dozing, he hears her slippers on the tile floor, the clink of her bangles rolling to her wrist, the tumble of pots and pans as she pulls one from the drying stack. She is going to boil water for oats.

At this thought, he gets up. The sun shines directly in his eyes. Many times he has told her he wants a double-egg omelet and butter-cooked potatoes for breakfast, but she continues to make oats, like she did every morning for her elderly father. But that man is old. What is he, PT Sir? A young man. A man of vigor and power.

Well, today, he is going to buy himself the breakfast he deserves. It will be even better than omelet-potatoes. Off he goes to the marketplace, where a sweet shop makes kochuri with chholar dal for breakfast. Fried dough, stuffed with green peas, and a lentil curry. A breakfast of decadence. Let his wife eat her oats!

On the street, a stray dog ambles after him, and he shoos it away.

"Go, hut!"

But the dog follows him, its ribs outlined in its skin, a patch of fur missing, its tongue hanging out of its pink mouth.

PT Sir dares to pick up a stick from the road and swat it at that dog. Only when he throws the stick does the dog retreat, trotting away in the other direction.

PT Sir has sent a dozen men to jail, does anybody know that? So this street dog better beware of him, or he can have it locked up in a snap of his fingers, ha-ha!

*

ONE MORNING, DAYLIGHT FAILS. The sky turns so dark that lights are flipped on throughout the neighborhood, lending the dawning of day a mood of dusk. With a storm that thunders and blazes, and whose rain strikes rooftops across the city, the monsoon arrives. PT Sir's wife draws the windows closed before the slanting rain, and PT Sir emerges from the house with his trousers folded up to his calves, his feet in rubber slippers. His work shoes he carries in a plastic bag.

From his doorstep, PT Sir surveys the terrain. Brown water sloshes this way and that, the street turned into a stream, as office-goers wade. PT Sir spots a rickshaw churning water as it makes its way slowly down the lane. It has high wheels, and a high blue seat sheltered under an accordion roof. When he raises an arm and calls, "Rickshaw!" the driver pedals toward him and comes to a lazy stop. With his shirt unbuttoned and calves muscled, his head dry under an umbrella held upright by the handlebars, the man looks blankly ahead and quotes a fare that is triple what it should be. PT Sir, with some pride, casually agrees to it.

"Fine," he says, "fine, let's go."

*

FOR YEARS, THE SCHOOL has tried to get the drainage in the access lane fixed so that it doesn't flood. Every monsoon, it floods. So it has today too. Students, in school uniform and Hawaii slippers, hover by the dry mouth of the lane, on high ground. Rainwater has flooded the underground dens of cockroaches, and now the insects emerge from cracks in the pavement. On land they dash, alarming girls who yell and stomp them dead. When a school bus arrives, or a classmate's car pauses, girls pile into the vehicle to be carried to the gate of the school.

Classes proceed as usual, but whose mind can be on Mongol invasions and trigonometry when the city is flooded? All day rain drips and drops, and when it pauses for a breath, it is replaced by the false rain of fat water from ledges and leaves.

In his class, PT Sir has them do yoga indoors, four students at a time, because it turns out that's how

many yoga mats there are. The others "meditate"—
eyes half-open, a giggle spreading now and then. PT
Sir says, "Quiet!" but he knows this too: The rules are
different on a rainy day.

*

AT LUNCHTIME THE PRINCIPAL, in a show of solidar-
ity, leaves her air-conditioned office and sits with the
teachers. She too has arrived with feet soaked, the
bottom of her sari darkened by water.

"Undignified," comments an English teacher. "All
of us teachers lifting up our saris like that to walk to
school. Imagine how it looks to the students!"

"It gives a poor impression to the parents," agrees
the maths teacher.

The principal, before a tiffin box of sandwiches,
teases, "PT Sir, we have all seen that you know powerful people."

PT Sir looks up from his lunch of noodles. He
smiles, and makes no protest.

"Any chance," the principal says, "something can
be done for our lane?"

*

SO IT IS THAT the following Monday, two laborers
appear, wearing city corporation badges, and present
themselves to the principal. "Your work order," they
say, offering her a sheet of much-folded paper. "Work
has been done. Sign and give back, please."

The principal cannot believe her eyes. "I noticed,"
she says, "that the lane looked dug up."

And here it is, indeed, a document detailing what has been done. Over the weekend, men dispatched by the municipal corporation ripped up the asphalt, pumped the old drainage pipes clean of muck and plastic, then sealed the road above.

The next time it rains, students and teachers walk down the school lane, clean and dry, while districts of the city drown.

LOVELY

AT THE END OF A CLASS, MR. DEBNATH IS SITTING IN his chair with a puddle of tea on a saucer, and he is blowing *phoo phoo*. I am analyzing my performance that I was recording on my phone. On the wall, some brown flowers are hanging around the faces of his late parents. High time for Mr. Debnath to buy fresh flowers.

"Lovely, today I am realizing," he is saying, after the others have left, "that you are growing far beyond this class."

"Don't say such things, please," I am protesting, even though I am secretly thinking that maybe he is right. My performances are always outshining. In fact, I am having the same thought myself. But I am always being humble. "I have to learn a lot more from you," I am saying to him.

"I have been writing a script, Lovely," he is saying. "Remember how I was getting a chance to go to Bombay, twenty years back? From that time till now, I have been writing this script. And it is getting to the point where I am thinking about casting and so on and so forth."

"Wow!" I am saying with my neck coming out like a goose. "You are directing a film?"

"Writing," he is saying, "and directing, naturally. Now, I have one question for you."

And just like that, with his tea breath on my face, he is asking me to be the heroine. The question is coming as such a shock I am taking one minute to understand fully what he is asking.

"Do you accept?" he is saying.

I am just looking at him like a fool. I am meaning *Yes! Yes! Yes!*

Mr. Debnath is telling me, "You must be wondering who is playing the lead opposite you? The hero, well, I am really writing that role for someone like Shah Rukh Khan."

"Shah Rukh Khan!" I am finally saying. My voice is catching in my throat. "Was I ever telling you that I am sleeping every night under a poster of Shah Rukh Khan?"

It is really too much emotion. I am feeling like I am on top of a high Himalayan peak of happiness. If I am having to be putting words to this feeling, that is truly how I am feeling.

"Someone *like* Shah Rukh Khan," Mr. Debnath is saying, "more or less."

But I am not even hearing.

"Accept?" I am saying. "Mr. Debnath, this is the greatest day of my life!"

JIVAN

IN THE BEGINNING, THE HOT AIR OF THE KITCHEN made my head swoon. Once I paused my work of flipping ruti and, recalling what I learned in PT class, lowered my head between my knees. Soon after, a guard, a man, noticed the slowed production line and said, in my ear, "Want to rest? I can take you to the clinic if you want."

Everybody knew what happened in the on-site clinic to women who were sedated and weak, unable to do more than lift a hand or briefly open their eyes.

No longer am I that light-headed woman. Every morning and every evening, I make more than a hundred pieces of ruti. My movements have become economical—slap and turn, pinch and lift. My head is down, my bony fingers swift. Looking at me, you might think I have become a servant, but that is true only of my hands. In my mind, I have resisted being imprisoned. In my mind, every morning I dress smartly, clip on my badge, and take the bus to my job at Pantaloons. That morning will come again. The clock, though reluctant, moves forward.

*

I HAVE ALWAYS BELIEVED in work. Only once, I promise Purnendu, only once did I think about committing a crime.

In the big city, one of the first things I noticed was how everybody had big cell phones like handheld televisions. One of those cell phones could pay for a few months of my father's medicines.

"So you stole a phone?" Purnendu says. He sits cross-legged on top of the bench, wearing office pants which smell like ironing. "From who?"

"No, wait," I say. "Listen first."

One day, on the main street, I saw a woman whose purse was unzipped. A wallet peeked out. The woman was holding a receipt and looking hopefully at the roll shop. My heart pounded in my ears as I reached forward and touched that wallet. I touched it gently at first, then nearly lifted it from the purse. Even while I was holding the wallet, indecision screamed at me: Should I really do this? Was I a thief? In any case, the wallet had caught on something deep in the purse. I tugged once, then let it go.

No, I wasn't a thief.

No, I was never a thief, but the woman turned around, surprised, and gripped my wrist. With my bony wrist in her strong hand, she shouted, "What are you doing?"

Everybody at the roll shop looked at me. The man who was cracking eggs on the black pan paused. The boy who was chopping onions held his rag-wrapped knife still in the air.

I looked at the ground, my wrist still in the hand of the woman. How soft her hand was. I readied for a beating.

But the woman with the soft hands bent toward me and asked me a question, her voice suddenly different.

"How old are you, child?" she said. "Are you hungry?"

The kindness of her voice made me harden with suspicion. Why was she being nice? I refused to speak, turning my eyes to the road, where yellow Ambassador taxis rumbled along, honking their horns.

"Why didn't you ask me for something to eat?" she said.

She took her roll from the shop, bought me one, and took me back to her office, me agreeing to her soft hand on my back, her warm fingers touching my skin through the zipper fallen open, in my mouth delicious chicken, nothing more. Her office was up an elevator. The box moved, and I kept a hand on the wall.

"Never been in a lift?" said the lady. She smiled. "Don't be afraid."

In the office, other ladies came forward and asked me many questions. After I devoured the chicken roll, one gave me two biscuits which I crammed in my mouth, buttery crumbs sticking to my chin.

They were an education NGO, and they provided scholarships for underprivileged children to attend one of the best schools in the area, S. D. Ghosh Girls' School.

*

ON THE PATH FROM our slum to my new school, there was a butcher shop. Every day I walked past skinned goats hanging from hooks, their bodies all muscle and fat except for the tails, which twitched. The goat must have had a life, much like me. At the end of its life, maybe it had been led by a rope to the slaughterhouse, and maybe, from the smell of blood which emerged from that room, the goat knew where it was being taken.

Before I began going to the good school, I used to feel that way. In this prison, sometimes, I feel it again.

But at that time, with my clean school uniform, a bag full of photocopied books strapped to my shoulders, even a new pencil in my pocket, I did not feel like that goat anymore.

*

THAT DOES NOT MEAN school was easy. I kept my distance, or others kept their distance from me, and from their faces I knew they found something physically unappealing about me: my hair, often knotted and chalky with dust, or my smell, like metal. But it did not keep me from laughing at what they said, accepting a glance thrown my way as a kind of friendship.

I learned English, the language of progress. I couldn't get anywhere if I didn't speak English, even I knew that. But I dreaded being asked to stand up and read from the textbook.

I read like this: "Gopal li-li-livaid—*lived* on a mou-mou-moonten, and he—"

The other girls, from middle-class homes where they read English newspapers and watched Hollywood films, disdained me. But in the slum, I was the only one with an English textbook, and who cared whether I was good or not? It was a place where most could not read a word—Bengali or English—and what I had was a great skill.

PT SIR

IN AUTUMN, DURING THE DURGA PUJO FESTIVAL, young lovers roam the streets, holding hands, till dawn. Ceremonial smoke wafts where priests worship, and drummers keep their beat going until the next day arrives. The streets, closed to cars, fill with vendors of fried snacks and cotton candy. Some neighborhoods install Ferris wheels and swinging pirate boats where traffic might have been.

On such a night, while the city celebrates, the Jana Kalyan Party leader, whom PT Sir has only briefly met, a man with three mobile phones in his palms at all times, dies. It is late, well after dinner, when PT Sir gets the phone call. His wife, woken by the ring of the phone, and worried by the tone of voice she hears, rises from bed and asks, "What happened?"

She tells him where he might be able to buy a grief wreath, of white evening flowers, at this hour.

PT Sir takes a rickshaw, then a taxi, then abandons the car and runs when the traffic stalls. Crowds stream past him in the opposite direction. Now and then a child, no taller than his hip, blows a pipe whose neck unfurls and reveals a feather.

The party leader's house is in the old part of the city, where lanes accommodate one Ambassador car at a time. Two police jeeps try to regulate the crowd, a mass of men holding hot earthen cups of tea by the cool rim. On balconies along the lane, neighbors watch the gathering like it is a festival of its own.

"Have they brought the body from the hospital?" PT Sir asks a stranger beside him, a man carrying a cloth bag like a scholar.

"Few minutes ago," he replies.

PT Sir sees no familiar faces, so he stands some distance from the house, holding a tall bunch of white flowers, the only flowers he could find at that hour. Murmurs spread that the chief minister is coming to pay his respects, and the railway minister too. A car is allowed through, bearing a famous actor, who steps out in sunglasses. To the crowd, he joins his hands and bows his head. Then he disappears inside the house. The crowd roars and moves as one, and for a moment PT Sir fears a stampede.

"Please keep order," shouts a man from the front. "His wife is inside, his elderly mother is inside, have respect for them!"

PT Sir feels ashamed of himself, a participant in this strangely excited crowd of the supposedly grieving. He feels the way he did at the first Jana Kalyan Party rally he attended, when he was a diffident man.

Should he go home? Should he, at a calmer

moment, phone the bereaved? But he has brought these flowers. Wouldn't he like to show Bimala Pal that he has come? There, inside the house, all the senior ministers are gathered. Wouldn't it be good to be acquainted with one or two of them?

At that moment he hears a voice.

"You have come," says the assistant, the same one who delivers PT Sir's courthouse bonuses by motorcycle. PT Sir follows him gratefully. The man leads him through the crowd—"Side, side," he commands—and PT Sir feels eyes on him. He can feel the crowd thinking, reminding him of that long ago moment on the train when he received free muri, who is this VIP?

LOVELY

WHEN THERE ARE NO BABIES OR NEWLYWEDS TO bless, the sisters of my hijra house are giving blessings for money on the local trains. It is our tradition, and we are doing it more during Durga Pujo days, when the goddess is not in the sky but here in our city.

"Come now, sisters," Arjuni Ma is saying to everyone in the compartment, clapping her palms together, "don't you want your day to be blessed?"

The passengers hiding by the windows are trying to look outside and ignore, but they cannot. Arjuni Ma is specifically calling to them. "Listen, mother, give us a few rupees from the goodness of your heart."

Every face that is turning to me, I am hoping it is not somebody from Mr. Debnath's acting class. Please god, I am thinking. Now I am on my way to being a star, why to ruin that reputation? Those classmates are maybe the only people in my life who have not seen me in this trade. They have not seen how this trade is making me a little disgusting in the eyes of others. But if I am not having this trade, how am I saving money for acting classes?

I am always learning from the train. Here is a mother sitting cross-legged with her baby sleeping in her lap. Her head is tilting on her shoulder and she is sleeping also, dead to the world. She is not hearing any of our words. Next time when I am having a role as a tired mother, I will be thinking about her.

A lot of people are looking outside, to the fields of their country, the soothing green outside the window. The fields of paddy and coconut trees, the endless green of the rural parts. Oh, fantasy! They are actually looking at the ugly suburbs. Banners are hanging above a lane, advertising cold cream. The cloth of the banners is poked with holes for letting the wind through. In quiet towns, two-story houses painted such colors like you may never see in the city—bright blue and yellow! pink and green!—are jutting up from dust, some with flags of the local political party, and one with a stray man on the roof, sent up to fix the satellite dish, scratching his head at the sky.

All this I am seeing through the windows of the train, like they are a kind of television.

*

THE INVITATION CARD IS arriving one morning, passed from hand to hand because there is no address on it except *Lovely Hijra, near Kolabagan Railway Station.* I am opening the card as if it is a flap of my heart. I am reading the words so many times I am knowing them like a song. Opening and closing the card, opening and closing the card—I am ready for my heart to be tearing at the fold.

On the given day, I am shampooing in the cold water of the municipal tap, oiling my elbows, putting some rose water on my face, putting a garland around the thick bun high on my head, and then I am setting out for the event hall where Azad is going to marry a woman. A real woman, with whom he is someday having children, just like I was pushing him to do. His days of being with a he-she like me are over. In my armpit I am holding a nicely wrapped box with a small European-looking statue inside.

The hall is having a flower-and-leaf gate spelling out in front: *Azad weds Shabnam*. A lady standing over there is giving every guest a cup of cool rose-flavored Rooh Afza.

I am slurping it down, so thirsty I am suddenly feeling. Still my tongue is feeling thick, my throat is feeling dry. Inside, Azad and his bride are sitting on matching thrones. Behind the thrones there is a heap of big wrapped boxes—must be they are toasters, blankets, dinner plates. Azad is smiling with all thirty-two teeth and shaking some old uncle's hand. Then he is seeing me, and we are going on looking at each other. We are having no words.

I was the one who was telling Azad to move forward and marry a woman, am I not remembering? But now Azad is looking handsome. His hair is nicely combed, and he is wearing an ivory dhoti kurta. His bride's face is powdered white like a ghost, and her lips are red like a tomato. On her neck she is wearing at least five–six gold necklaces. I am not caring about gold, but I am caring, with my empty Rooh Afza cup in my hand, that Azad was buying these for her with love. Wasn't Azad once telling me that he could not live without me? So why was he not marrying some ugly one-eyed person?

Anyway, I am having to be noble now. I am going up to the bride and groom with my gift.

"Lovely," Azad is saying uncomfortably, "good that you came."

I am feeling like I will cry. While my heart is bouncing like a Ping-Pong ball inside my chest, I am saying to them, "Long married life to both of you." The girl is bending low, wanting to be blessed, and I, Lovely, am feeling like a kind of goddess, a kind of saint, believing when you love him let him go.

In the dinner line, one eye on the biryani and one eye on the Chinese chili chicken, I am not knowing whether to laugh or cry. Look at me, waiting for the feast at my husband's marriage. With my plate and napkin in one hand, chomping chomping, I am looking around at the hall, decorated with plastic flowers, a small fountain in one corner. Isn't this life strange?

My love for Azad, I am telling myself, is existing in some other world, where there is no society, no god. In this life we were never getting to know that other world, but I am sure it is existing. There, our love story is being written.

At the end of the night, when I am walking down

the lane, all the shops are shuttered other than a welder's shop where a masked man is working. From the machine, bright sparks are falling on the road. In the hands of this tired man, it is like Diwali.

*

MR. DEBNATH IS TELLING me to have a demo video prepared so I can be showing my reel to his movie's producers, and starting to get small, small projects on my own also. At one demo office, the front desk man's mouth is hanging open, and he is poking inside his mouth with a toothpick. This is the cheapest place I could be finding, so I am having to make my demo video here, no question.

"Which level," the man is saying dully.

"What?"

"Which level demo video you are wanting? Basic level six hundred rupees, better variety a thousand rupees, deluxe package twenty-five hundred rupees."

I am gulping to hear the prices. Then I am choosing basic level. When he is filling out a form on a clipboard, he is asking, "What is your name?"

"Lovely," I am saying.

At this he is snorting like a horse.

When I am looking at the form, I am seeing that he is writing next to my name: *B.*

"Why you are marking me *B* already?" I am demanding. "I didn't even perform."

"Calm down, madam," the man is complaining. "Why are you looking at what I am writing? It's just lingo, nothing personal about you."

But he is not telling me what it is meaning. I am learning later, on my own. B-class. An actor who is not having the pretty face or light skin color for A-class roles. B-class actor is someone who is only playing a servant, a rickshaw puller, a thief. The audience is wanting to see B-class actors punched and slapped and defeated by the hero.

I am going to a room and standing nervously in front of not a theoretical camera but a real camera. It is balanced on top of a tripod, and there is a blinking red light on it. The man with sleepy eyes is standing behind it, and even though I am not liking him and he is not liking me, I am feeling like a real actress. I am looking at the lens and knowing—through this lens, someday I am reaching a thousand people, a million people. So what if there is only one grumpy man here, and he is receptionist and clerk and cameraperson also? It may be a boutique company, as they say.

The man is telling me that he will give me a fifteen-minute reel with different characters and looks. That is what I am getting for six hundred, he is reminding me.

"Now, if you are taking the deluxe package—"

"No need!" I am saying. "Basic package is okay for me."

I am tying up my hair and doing some voice exercises. In this empty room, my voice is sounding hollow.

Now he is saying, "Can you do an angry house-wife?"

Then: "Now you try a person waiting for the bus and it is just not coming. Subtle expressions, see?"

Then: "You are a baby throwing a tantrum," to which I am saying, "A baby?"

But maybe these are tests for being an actress. You have to slide into the character, no hesitation.

I am lying down on a dirty mattress laid on the floor anyhow. A small worm is running along the edge of the mattress, trying to find an opening where it can be hiding. I am lying on my back with my hands and feet up, more like a dying cockroach than a baby. I am wailing *waan waan*.

The whole time, I am feeling like the man is secretly filming me for a bad website. How is it that this cashier is having full control of the camera? It is giving me an uneasy feeling in my chest.

When the man is taking six hundred and forty rupees from me—"tax," he is explaining—and giving me the CD, I am feeling somehow cheated.

*

WHEN I AM COMING back home, there is one man waiting in front of my door. He is suited-booted, and everybody is looking at him because his clothes are looking too clean. On his fingers he is wearing one green stone, one red stone, one blue stone, some copper rings.

"Is your name Lovely?" he is saying, as I am taking my key out of my purse.

"What is it to you?" I am saying. Men are always wanting things.

"Jivan said," he is gulping, like a nervous fish, "Jivan said you are willing to come to the court, her mother came and saw you—"

"Who are you, mister?" I am asking him.

Then he is saying, "I am Jivan's lawyer. I just need to confirm that you will come to the court."

He is giving me a form.

"I am not knowing how to read English," I am telling him.

"But she was teaching you?" he is asking.

"She was teaching me," I am sighing. "How is Jivan? Is she getting proper food?"

Instead of answering my question, this man is liking to ask more questions. Now he is saying, "Can I sit and talk with you? I can help you fill this out. Maybe at the tea shop over there?"

PT SIR

TWO MONTHS AFTER BIMALA PAL BECOMES, QUIETLY and without ceremony, Jana Kalyan Party's new leader, she sends PT Sir on a mission that, if PT Sir is being honest, he finds a little bewildering.

A winter chill is in the air when a party jeep takes PT Sir to a village called Chalnai, eighty kilometers away. On the highway, large trucks transporting the season's vegetables—cauliflower, potatoes—blow musical horns. Pedestrians, visible as triangles of wool shawls on two legs, run across the highway now and then, fearing nothing.

Nearing the village, the jeep slows as its wheels crush grain placed on the road by villagers. A girl sits on the pads of her feet, supervising the use of passing cars as millstones. Behind her, fields of stubble roll from the edge of the paved road to a horizon where woods blur.

In Chalnai, the government school is a doorless structure next to a dust field. Inside, a dozen men and women—teachers, PT Sir understands—sit cross-legged on the floor. When PT Sir enters, the teachers say nothing. They have about them an air of waiting to be instructed what to do, how to behave, whether to speak or smile. PT Sir joins his hands in greeting.

PT Sir's task is to impress upon the teachers that students must have a half hour of physical activity every day. They must be let loose from their books to eat the air, play a sport, or run races. If the school lacks large grounds, the students must be allowed to jump rope. After twenty minutes of lecturing, during which PT Sir feels slightly absurd, he distributes among the teachers pamphlets from the party, with illustrations showing overworked students choosing to hang themselves or jump from the roof. It has happened. It is a serious problem. But here, with the blank-faced teachers nodding at everything he says, PT Sir feels himself sent on a silly mission. This, after all, is a village, with abundant fields and woods where children run wild.

At night, at home with his wife, he takes off a shirt and undershirt going red from the soil of the region. When he washes his face, the red dust is in the crooks of his ears.

"So why did they *really* send you to this place?" demands his wife.

PT Sir thinks about this. He feels that this field trip was some kind of test, but whether he has passed or not, he does not yet know.

JIVAN

BEHIND THE MAIN PRISON BUILDING THERE IS A long gutter, green with growth. Running above it is a crooked water pipe with a dozen faucets. Here I kneel every other morning, and wash clothes for Americandi.

One morning, I am kneeling and scrubbing, I am beating the kameez and salwar against the ground, watching a circle of foam spread, when I feel somebody behind me. It is a guard, who says, "Your lawyer is here. Leave that and come."

Is it so easy? Don't I know that Americandi will punish me for leaving her clothes unwashed?

Rapidly I rinse and wring, putting my weight into my arms, the wrung clothes releasing ropes of water. I flap the clothes in the air, a gentle rain falling back toward me, and hang them up to dry on a clothesline inside my cell. When I walk, finally, to the visiting room, with each step my back aches like its hinges need oiling.

*

I HAVE NEVER SEEN Gobind smile so wide.

"Lovely is here," he says, standing up when he sees me, "you are right. The message has been delivered."

"I know," I tell him. "My mother found her, when you couldn't!"

"She has promised she will testify," he says, as if he can't hear me. "A win for us!"

A few days later, in the papers, I see stories which claim Gobind did extensive on-the-ground investigation, endless nights of detective work, to track down the elusive hijra, Lovely.

*

WHEN I SPEAK ABOUT PT Sir, Purnendu raises his eyebrows.

"What?" I say. "Do you know him?"

"Is this the man who has been seen with Bimala Pal?" Purnendu says. "The new member of Jana Kalyan Party?"

"No, no," I tell him. "He was just my PT teacher at S. D. Ghosh School."

*

ONE DAY, AFTER A CLASS during which the sun made me feel faint, PT Sir called me. What was wrong now? I wondered. My hem fraying, my shoelaces soiled? But he said, in a scolding tone so as not to embarrass me, "Are you eating properly?"

I tried to smile, as if it was a silly concern. "It was too hot, sir, that's why I felt weak."

He looked at me for a while, and I waited to be punished. When teachers called me, that was usually what happened.

But PT Sir took me up to the staff room, and handed me a tiffin box from his bag. Inside, there were several pieces of ruti folded in triangles, and vegetables.

"Sit and eat it," he said. I did, all those pipes in me clamoring for food, their need louder than my embarrassment. My mother always cooked food for us, but that month, my father needed an injection which cost us our grocery money. I had only eaten some rice and salt for breakfast.

After that, PT Sir kept an eye on me. He slipped me some bread and jam, or a banana. I, in turn, participated enthusiastically in his class. I jogged in place—"High knee! Low!"—and bounced a basketball with vigor. I jumped toward the new hoops. I raced with my elbows slicing the air and my thighs pumping. I thought of all the times I had stayed home to look after my father, and now, my sweat shined on my limbs.

PT Sir, with his balding head ringed by a patch of combed hair, stood in the sun class after class, a whistle ready at his lips. He smiled at me and told me, "Well done!"

Once, he asked me if I was interested in going to a cricket camp.

I wondered sometimes if he paid attention to me because he felt like an outsider too. He was a father,

I imagined, and all the other teachers were mothers. When the principal spoke about morals at the morning assembly, and the microphone began to screech, the ladies looked around for PT Sir. Such was his place in the school, a little apart from everybody else.

*

THEN TWO THINGS HAPPENED.

One, I went to a classmate's birthday party. Priya's mother took us home in a bus, and paid for my bus fare. I stood on the uneven wooden planks, this time in shoes, reaching high for the bar that ran along the ceiling. A lady was eating chocolate wafers, and had a full bag in her lap. I looked at the chocolates, sitting ignored, nobody wanting them.

In Priya's room, she had a desk for working and a special lamp just for the desk, which curved downward to put light on the book but not in her eyes. I had never seen a lamp like it. I still covet it.

In the kitchen, Priya crushed biscuits and chocolate sauce to make a sweet dish that her mother scolded her for making, as it would spoil our appetite for the dinner. But I ate spoonfuls of it, and then ate my fill at dinner. I had never seen such a spread. There was luchi, dal, chicken, but also Chinese noodles from the cart at the bus stop, in case we did not find the home-cooked food delicious. When I left, Priya's mother gave me a tiffin box full of food for my mother and father. Was Priya a millionaire? No, she was only middle class.

It made me proud. Look at me, Ma, with my middle-class friend. That's what I thought. One day I would be middle class too.

*

THE SECOND EVENT HAPPENED one night, when I was woken by my mother shouting. It was dark, and I rose in a panic.

"Look how they scratched me, those savages," my mother was saying, holding out a bare forearm. And they had, whoever they were. I climbed off the bed, my breath catching, and held her arm tenderly, as if my touch could soothe. A small circle of potential customers stood around, bereft of breakfast, agitated by the event they had stumbled upon.

At the nighttime market, two or three men had shoved my mother, grabbed her grocery-shopping money from her fist, and shouted at her to "go back to Bangladesh."

Later, when the audience had dispersed, Ma sat in the house with her head in her hands. When she looked up, after long minutes, she said, "They were touching me *here,* touching me *here*. Oh my girl, my gold, don't make me tell you."

I saw my mother then as a woman. I felt her humiliation. And where I had always felt shame, I now felt white-hot anger. Anger crept into my jaws and I had to gnash my teeth to be calm.

Why was this our life? What kind of life was it, where my mother was forced to buy cheap vegetables in the middle of the night, and got robbed and attacked for it? What kind of life did we have, where my father's pain was not taken seriously by a doctor until it was too late?

So I made a decision. Whether it was a good decision or a bad decision, I no longer know.

INTERLUDE

BRIJESH, ASPIRING ACTOR,
VISITS A NEW MALL

A NEW MALL OPENED WHERE THE SEWING MACHINE factory used to be. My jaw dropped when I saw it. It looked like an airport. Sharp and spiky. Glass here, glass there. Lights everywhere, like it was festival time.

On Sunday, after the acting class, I put on my new jeans and buttoned up my shirt with a horseman stitched on the chest pocket—Playboy shop in Allen Lane, go there sometime—then took out my phone and called my friend Raju, who does house-painting work. Together we went. Outside the mall, there were the snack boys and syrup-ice boys, and a few of them I knew so I nodded to them and they said, "Go inside, go inside, see how it is!"

So Raju and I went. Raju had some paint on his arms. My hair was washed and combed. My shoes were a bit dirty, but I had put polish on top of the dirt and covered it up, almost. Then we stood in the line for the metal detector, and I looked up at the big posters of ladies wearing golden watches. Then we walked through the metal detector, and at this point I could smell the AC air coming from inside, with a smell of perfumes and leather bags also. Oh that cool air on my face. I felt good. I felt excited. The cool, cool breeze coming, when suddenly the guard caught my arm.

"Fifty rupees," the guard said.

"What?" I said. "Go away, old man." Can't believe how anybody just asks for money, no excuse needed! I should also stand outside a mall and shout out amounts of money. See what I can get.

"Fifty rupees admission," said the guard, neither annoyed nor interested, his eyes looking somewhere else.

"Admission to go to where? We're just going to the shops," said Raju, taking out his big new smartphone and holding it casually, just to show that he is a moneyed man.

But the old guard was not fooled. "See, brother," he began, "fifty rupees and you can go in. Otherwise, you enjoy the air outside.

"Like me," he added, but I did not have a mood to feel friendship with him.

"But you didn't take admission from that aunty!" argued Raju. The woman ahead of us, her soft white belly spilling over the waist of her pink sari, her elbows disappearing in folds of fat, a woman who surely eats mutton every day, she had already disappeared in the mall.

"Do I make the rules, brother?" said the guard.

"I am just telling you what is what. Now you want to quarrel with me and say, this person, that person! So what will I do? I am just telling you what is the rule. Now you decide—"

So Raju and I stepped away from the entrance. We looked at each other. Neither of us wanted to say it. So Raju clapped my back and I smacked his shoulder, and we went to the syrup-ice stall and had some orange syrup-ice. Then we went back to work. Him to his house painting, that paint-smelling turban on his head again. Me to my electrician's shop. It was giving me pain in my wrist, pain in my thumb. At least the syrup-ice was delicious.

PT SIR

IN COURT FOR WHAT WILL BE HIS LAST CASE, PT SIR
faces a counterfeiter, a man who sells fake Nikees and
Adidavs to the local malls. His name, PT Sir reminds
himself from a chit of paper before taking the stand,
is Azad.

The man looks suspect, that's what PT Sir thinks.
There is something too new about his clothes. His
hair is smoothed back with gel. Is he wearing eye-
liner? Could be. PT Sir has been told he is a counter-
feit goods trader, an immoral man who is harming
the national economy and deserves to be jailed. That
is the charge with which they have brought him to
court today.

"Where do you get your supply?" says the judge.

"Judge sir," says Azad. "Believe me, this is all
made up. I can't even—"

"Where?" repeats the judge. "You want to go to
jail for this?"

"I don't know what you are saying, judge sir," protests Azad. "I am only transporting what the boss
man tells me, I don't know real weal, fake shake—"

"Who has brought the charge?" says the judge, exasperated. The lawyer points out PT Sir. He takes the stand. He tells his story: He bought shoes for eight hundred rupees, then after one walk found that the sole was ungluing from the shoe.

"Who are you, mister?" interrupts Azad. He is listening, wide-eyed. "Who is this man? I have never seen him in my life. What is your issue with me?"

The judge warns Azad to be quiet. In the end, the judge orders Azad to pay a fine of five thousand rupees.

PT Sir looks at the man, and is shocked to see his eyes are wet. Azad is crying. In a panic, he wails, "Judge sir, I am just a transport man, where will I find five thousand rupees? I just got married, I have a wife to support now—"

The judge, irritated, announces that a trade in fake goods will not be tolerated, not while he has a courtroom to preside over. "If you cannot pay the fine, you can serve a jail term," he declares. "Is that what you choose?"

LOVELY

NOW THAT I AM OWNING A DEMO VIDEO, ON MR. DEB-nath's recommendation I am visiting a casting director, Mr. Jhunjhunwala.

Morning of the appointment, I am putting baby powder on my oily spots—forehead, nose, chin. Just in case he is asking me to film something right there!

Once again I am going to the film district, but this time I am going in the opposite direction from Mr. Debnath's house. I am passing by a big studio, built a hundred years ago, which is now blocking part of the road. Since big-big stars are filming in that studio, the municipal corporation is letting the studio stay.

The casting director's office is not far. I am walking down a lane where there is an open gutter thick with mosquitoes, and soon I am seeing a door that is saying *Jhunjhunwala*.

The door is thin, and one plank of wood is splintered at the bottom. Along the stairway, I am feeling surprised to see red splashes of spit which are soiling the walls. To be truthful, this office is looking quite dirty, but who am I to know where fame and success are coming from?

I am knocking on door 3C, hearing the loud voice of a man on the phone inside. The man is calling, "Come, come." Inside, the man's head is bent to the phone, and he is waving me forward, showing me the two chairs on the other side of his table. I am sitting, touching the edge of my blouse on my shoulder to make sure the bra strap is tucked inside. Mr. Debnath has prepared me to always sit straight and tall. The pose is making me feel confident when I am actually feeling nervous. Then I am waiting, trying to look a bit humble and a bit royal.

The phone conversation is finally ending, and Mr. Jhunjhunwala is standing up, coming around to my side, and taking my hand in both of his hands. He is shaking my hand like I am the prime minister.

"Forgive me for keeping you waiting," he is saying. When he is speaking, a scent of paan is coming from his mouth. I can see his teeth are red from betel stains, so maybe he is the one spitting in the stairs every day. "Some producers, they depend a lot on me, and want to discuss every small detail . . ." He is shaking his head. What to do with these needy producers!

"Chai? Pepsi?" he is offering, and a small boy is poking his head in through the door to take the order. How he is knowing that he is needed, I don't know. But this is a professional film office, so this is how things are run in an office. I am saying water only, thank you, but Mr. Jhunjhunwala is saying, "Only water?" And then he is telling the boy, "Bring a cold Pepsi, straight from the fridge."

So I am drinking Pepsi from a glass bottle, keeping the thin straw in one corner of my mouth like film stars do. I am not wanting to spoil my lipstick. In front of me, there is a table topped with a glass slab, and under that glass slab are autographed postcards by big movie stars. Some of the names I am recognizing. Are they prints or originals? I am thinking. And then I am scolding myself—look at me, so cynical! Of course they are originals. This is the society in which I move about now.

Then Mr. Jhunjhunwala is sitting down, with his chai in front, and he is looking at me with a strict expression. "Now, your acting teacher, Mr. Debnath, is someone I respect very much. So I take it very seriously—very, very seriously!—when he says, look, here's a student I think you should meet. Immediately I said, it will be my honor, just tell her to come quickly."

I am smiling, sipping. The fizzy and sweet drink is making me feel good.

Mr. Jhunjhunwala is saying, "Now. Kamz, I mean, Kamal Banerjee, you have heard of him?"

Who has not heard of the great director Kamal Banerjee?

"So Kamz is casting for a film just now. Let me tell you the story. It will be a love story with a twist, set during a harvest season in which a whole village is suffering because too little rain, too few crops, you see, like that. It will be a blockbuster, mark my words.

Now, there is a scene in which a hijra, a bad luck hijra, comes to the village, saying, 'Give me money no, mother, please, my child is starving,' et cetera, okay? And our hero, who is suffering himself from his fields dying, mind you, in his suffering he comes out and chases away the hijra with a broom."

I am sucking my Pepsi too fast now. The main part is coming, surely.

"You," says Mr. Jhunjhunwala, "will be perfect for the hijra part. Do you have your demo CD with you?"

I am wanting to be a heroine on-screen. At least the heroine's sister or girlfriend. And here is the great casting director telling me about a minor role, where the character would be chased off-screen with a broom! I am putting the straw away from my lips. My heart is sinking, and all of a sudden this room is making me unhappy. I am seeing the mousehole in the corner. I am feeling the wobble in this old chair. I am saying in a tiny voice, "Yes, sir." I am handing him the CD in its case.

Mr. Jhunjhunwala is feeling the disappointment in my voice. He is taking the CD and leaning back in his chair. "You know," he is saying, looking at the ceiling, "many people come to me and think I can put them in a movie, instantly. But it doesn't work like that. If you are serious about your career, if you don't want to remain on an amateur level, then you have to start at the entry level."

"Yes, of course, sir," I am saying. "I did not mean— Oh I'm just learning how the business works! Forgive me for not knowing."

"No, there is nothing to forgive in not knowing," he is saying, feeling a bit friendly again. "Let me look at this CD, and then I will call you, fine? Please pay the hundred rupees fee on your way out."

"Fee!" I am saying in a feeble voice. "There is a fee?"

"Am I looking like a nonprofit agency to you, Lovely?" Mr. Jhunjhunwala is saying, smiling. "Yes, the fee is for keeping you in my roster, looking for roles for you."

When I am climbing down the stairs, belly full of Pepsi sloshing inside, I am feeling scammed. One, he was taking my hundred rupees, and two, I will never be getting a good role from him. Are all these men playing a joke on me?

Outside, the sun is too bright. I am holding a hand above my eyes. I was hearing once that Reshma Goyal, who is now such a big star, was plucked by a casting director at a Café Coffee Day. One cup of coffee there costs one hundred rupees. This thought is making me sigh. If I was rich, I could be chasing my dreams in that way also.

For a few minutes I am feeling so disheartened, all I am doing is walking down the street and scrolling through WhatsApp.

My sisters are forwarding me helpful advices.

Warning from All India Dieticians Professional Group: Do not eat orange and chocolate in the same day, otherwise—

Don't answer phone calls coming from num-

ber +123456; it is a way of using your SIM to call internationally—

One sister is sending me a joke.

Why is Santa Singh keeping a full glass and an empty glass beside his bed at night? Because he may or may not drink water!

I am looking up and seeing a boy at a corner shop. He is refilling someone's cell phone credit, scratching a card with his fingernail to get the code, but his eyes are straight on my breasts.

"Want to come drink my milk?" I am shouting.

Now I am close to the train station, but instead of taking the train, I am walking, walking, walking. My feet are turning left, right, left on their own, until I am standing in front of a house I am knowing very well. It is a two-story house, painted yellow. Azad's house. So what if he is married? He was the one telling me that our bond cannot be broken by man-made rules. But now it has been many days, he has not come to me only. I am wishing for his embrace now. I am wishing that he is coming to me again, and we are sitting on the floor eating chocolate ice cream. I can be telling him all about Mr. Jhunjhunwala. I know he will even be making me laugh about it.

He has been irritated by our marriage talk, that much I know. But he will come. I am looking at the balcony, eager to see a shirt or pant which is holding the shape of him. But the clothes strings are empty. There are only Azad's shoes drying against the balcony railing. Azad wore those shoes so much, I can recognize them from this distance also. It is this Nike brand, but it is better because, instead of one tick, it has two. Azad was always knowing the latest style. My heart is thinking of all those times he was opening those shoes inside my house, my room, and embracing me—

Suddenly a man is saying, "O ma, please to let the customers come." I am turning around. There is a vehicle repair garage behind me, smelling of diesel. The man who is talking to me is a Sikh uncle. He must be owning the repair garage. He is wearing a gray uniform and a red turban.

"Why?" I am demanding. "Am I an elephant that I am blocking the whole path? Your customers can't walk here if they want?"

But immediately I am having one frightening thought: I am not wanting Azad to accidentally see me like this. So I am sashaying away.

"Okay, uncle," I am saying. "You asked nicely, so I am gone."

JIVAN

UMA MADAM TAPS HER STEEL-TIPPED STICK AGAINST the bars of our cells. Down the corridor she goes, *clang clang clang.*

"Up, up," she calls. "Time to get up!"

I hear the sound coming closer. In front of my cell it stops. I look up from the mattress, where I have been, not asleep, but unwilling to begin the day. It is six in the morning, and the sun's heat has already warmed the walls and cooked the air. My skin sticks. When I raise my head, Uma madam points her stick through the bars. "Especially you!" she says. "Because of you we are having to take all this trouble. Why are you still sleeping?"

My case has brought scrutiny upon the women's prison. TV channels and filmmakers want to show how we live, what we do. I imagine them crawling inside, observing us like we are monkeys in a zoo: "Now the inmates have one hour to watch TV. Then they will cook the food." The more requests the administration denies, the more suspicious they look. The men and women of the administration protest that it is a matter of security and safety. But what does our prison have to hide? How bad are the conditions? The public wants to know. It is looking likely, we hear, that some TV requests will be granted. Before the camera crews appear, the prison must be "beautified."

"Beautification!" Uma madam scoffs as she walks away.

This morning, I receive the task of scrubbing decades of grease and black soot from the kitchen walls. Others mop and wipe the floors, replace light-bulbs, and plant saplings in the garden. A favored few do the gentle work of painting murals on the walls. Americandi, leader of all, sticks a melting square of Cadbury in her mouth and supervises.

*

THE WORK CAUSES old aches to flare. Throughout the week, women complain about the long hours on their feet. The steel wool and kerosene with which I scrub grease make my palm burn, but who knows if this hand, at this task, in this prison, is mine? In my mind, my hand grips the table in front of me in the courtroom, watching as my supporters—Kalu, with his neck tumor; Lovely, of course; some regular customers of my mother's breakfast business who have been asking her to reopen her morning shop—appear in the courtroom to tell all gathered that they have seen me taking books to Lovely. They know I teach her English. Lovely's neighbors know too. Isn't this, the knowledge of a dozen people, a kind of evidence?

*

THE NEXT TIME PURNENDU comes, I tell him about the day I told my mother I was quitting school.

"Ma," I said to her one day, "I will tell you something, but you can't be angry."

Purnendu leans forward, as if he is my mother.

She turned around from the stove, a flour-dusted ruti on her upturned palm, and looked at me.

"After class ten," I said, "I will leave school. I will work and support you and Ba."

My ears were hot. My mouth was dry.

"Who taught you these stupid things?" Ma said, looking up at me. "You want to leave school? Look at this smart girl! And do what?"

"Work, Ma, work!" I said. "Ba has not worked in so long, because his back is not healing. That nighttime market is not safe for you. Did you forget how you got attacked? How are we making money?"

"That's nothing for you to worry about," she snapped. "When did you become such a grandma? Just go to school, study hard, that is your job."

But I could not give up. If I let her talk me out of it, I would never attempt it again.

"Class ten graduates," I said, "can get well-paying jobs. I can finish class ten, sit for the board exams, then look for a job."

After days of back and forth, Ma gave up. One

night, as we were finishing our meal, she threw up her hands.

"Now this job ghost is sitting on your shoulder, what can I do?" she said. "So fine! Ruin your life, what do I care? Grow up and live in a slum, that will be good!"

Maybe that was a poor decision. But whom did I have to teach me how to build a better life?

*

IN THE MONTH LEADING up to the board exams, I studied hard. Late nights I sat on top of the high bed, a flashlight in one hand aimed at the page, my body swaying back and forth as I murmured paragraphs. As night grew deeper, in the silence around me, sometimes I heard a man pissing in the gutter right outside the house. Sometimes I heard footsteps, soft like a ghost's. I don't know how much I learned, but I did memorize whole textbooks by heart.

In March, the board exams began. I went to my assigned school building—we were given seats in different schools, away from our own, so that we could not scratch answers into our desks beforehand. A few girls were pacing in the lane, textbooks open in their arms, their lips moving. Some distance away, a girl was bent over and vomiting while her mother patted her back.

Inside, in a classroom, it was strange to take my chair, a sloping desk before it that belonged to somebody else. The desk was scratched with hearts which said S+K. Sheets of answer paper were passed out by a teacher, and I waited with my sheets, gripping my new ball pen, until the question paper was distributed. Outside the window a tree held still.

Three hours later, when the bell rang, I handed over my sheets, bound with an elastic string, to the invigilator. My middle finger was swollen with the pressure of the pen.

In the corridor, girls stood in clusters, hands smudged with ink, some rubbing their aching hands. I left, overhearing pieces of conversations.

"What did you write for the summer crops question?"

"Sorghum!"

"I *knew* this diagram would come."

*

ON THE DAY OF RESULTS, my heart leaped to see I had passed, with fifty-two percent. It was the poorest score in my class, and my classmates looked at me with concern. They expected me to cry, or collapse in despair. A few girls were standing in the corner, sniffling into handkerchiefs because they had received seventy percent. But unlike them, I was not planning to go to college. All I needed was to pass, and I had.

At home, I was feted as a graduate. How proud were my mother and father. In celebration, my mother pressed a milk sweet in my mouth, and distributed a packet of sweets to the neighbors.

"My daughter," she announced proudly, "is now class ten pass!"

It was as if she had forgotten my plan. I had not.

The week after, with a copy of my exam certificate in hand, I walked into the New World Mall and got a job, in the jeans section of Pantaloons.

*

AND THERE, AT PANTALOONS, I picked up a bad habit. Everyone around me had bad habits. We were earning our own money, why should we not indulge? I started smoking cigarettes. Costly cigarettes, branded singles which I bought with pride and lit from a slow-burning rope dangling from a corner of the shop. I held each cigarette between my fingers like a film star.

*

THE NIGHT THE TRAIN would burn, I walked to a place where my mother would not come upon me. The Kolabagan train station. There was a cigarette shop open there until late hours. I bought a single. I lit it. On the platform I stood like an independent woman, flicking ash. Next to me, I rested a package of my textbooks which I was long past needing. I would give them to Lovely.

A few of the passengers inside the halted train looked at me, all alone at night, smoking a cigarette. They were thinking, I thought, that I was a risky girl.

This is what city girls do, I thought. I enjoyed troubling them.

Then I heard two slaps of thunder. Quick as lightning, a crackle of fire spread through the train. I saw two shapes slipping away into the overgrown public garden next to the railway lines, the slum's toilet. One minute two coaches were smoking, a trembling fire within them, and the next the fire was roaring out of the windows, jumping from coach to coach. Other than the fire, I heard nothing, though I could see faces trapped and screaming. I stood, frozen, a tiny fire glowing in my hand. The air began to smell like burning hair.

Directly in front of me, locked in the train, a man was beating his wrist against the iron bars of a window. The man was looking at me. A grown man, he was looking at me and crying. He was speaking to me. Between his lips stretched saliva. I could not hear his words, but I could guess them. He was begging for help. He was holding up a little girl. She was struggling, squirming, crying.

He was pleading with me to come up and, somehow, grab his little girl, pull her through the window bars if I could.

I turned and ran. In a gutter somewhere, I dropped my cigarette. Then I ran and ran, and did not stop until I arrived home.

*

ALL I AM GUILTY OF, Purnendu, listen—all I am guilty of is being a coward.

PT SIR

ONE MORNING, AT THE SCHOOL ASSEMBLY, WHILE the principal speaks, the microphone shrieks.

Students cover their ears. Teachers keep sober faces.

Instead of hurrying forward to fix the problem, PT Sir stands with the other teachers, calmly sipping a cup of tea.

The principal calls, "Where is Suresh?"

Suresh is a peon in the administrative office. When he is fetched, he goes up to the microphone and jiggles the cables. He unplugs it and plugs it in once more. He taps the head of the microphone.

PT Sir looks on, not moving a finger.

JIVAN

THEN PURNENDU IS GONE. I WAKE WITH MY HEART clamoring in its cage. I force stale bread and dry potatoes down my throat—no tea today. The sun, unseen, makes itself felt in clothes sticking to our bellies and salt water dripping down our necks. Kneeling, I perform today's beautification task, which is to clean a bathroom. I scrub the toilet, and pour boric acid down a pipe. The acid, diluted in water, stings where my hand holds old cuts. But it will kill the moving, pulsing soil smeared in the sewage lines—dozens of cockroaches.

All the while, in a clean office far from here, Purnendu writes my story, and his editor makes it better.

"Your editor made the story better?" I laughed when Purnendu told me. "My story would be better if . . ."

I count on my hands. "If we had not been evicted, do you see? If my father had not broken his back, if my mother had not been attacked for trying to run a small business. If I could have afforded to finish school."

"Not better like that," said Purnendu.

"Then like what?"

He had no answer.

*

TWO DAYS LATER, I am standing in line for my morning meal, when Uma madam arrives in the courtyard, waving a newspaper in the air.

"You," she says, looking at me. Her mouth twists, hiding a smile. Then she hands me the newspaper. "Nice job."

The headline, in large text, reads, *"I THREW BOMBS AT THE POLICE": A TERRORIST TELLS HER LIFE STORY.*

The story begins: *Over several interviews conducted at the women's prison, this reporter heard a story of poverty and misfortune, as well as a lifelong anger at the government. It began when Jivan was a child, and was, along with her family, evicted from their settlement near Kurla mines. At that time, she freely confessed to this reporter, she and her family prepared homemade bombs with which they attacked the police.*

I move out of the line, and sit on the ground. I read the lines again. Did I forget to clarify to him that those bombs, as we called them, were nothing more than urine and shit? They were the pathetic defense of an insect.

I check the byline. *Purnendu Sarkar,* it reads. That was his name, wasn't it?

I read some more. *Her anger at the government is not recent, and has roots in a lifetime of neglect. From mistreatment of her father at a government hospital, leaving him with chronic debilitating pain as the result of a back injury, to her time living in government housing where an unreliable water supply made daily life difficult, close analysis of her story reveals animosity toward the government—*

I finish reading the article, and begin again. I finish it once more, and return to the top of the column, over and over until the words become no more than balls of earth rolled by termites. I close my eyes, and the ground tilts, taking me with it.

Uma madam takes the newspaper from me. I let her take it. From where I sit, I see only her feet, wrinkled skin in Bata slippers, and a sari reduced to rag in the humid air. "Feels good?" she taunts above my head. "This is what happens when you do secret interviews without permission! Do another! Do ten more! See how much they help!"

My head feels drawn to the earth, incapable of raising itself. So that is who he was, Purnendu. I listen to Uma madam's scolding in this posture of shame, until the posture is all I am.

*

MA COMES, holding a newspaper in her hand.

"Don't show that to me," I say, anger flaring at her.

She opens the leaves, turning the cottony pages one by one.

"Wait, wait," she says. "Kalu read this to me. He said it is good." She shows me a column inside, marked by pencil.

Beware of trial by media, says the article. This is a different paper. *Where is concrete proof that this young woman had involvement in the attack? Everything the police tells us is circumstantial evidence. The woman is being sacrificed because of her Muslim identity.*

"See?" says my mother. "Kalu told me this newspaper is speaking up in your defense. People are listening. Nothing is decided yet. Don't give up hope."

I don't know what this means, this matter of hope. Moment by moment, it is difficult to know whether I have it, or not, or how I might tell.

"This just means you are being hopeless," my mother teases. Then she smiles, and touches my cheek while the guard has her back turned to us.

There is nothing funny, but my mother's smile, those familiar folds of her mouth, that crooked tooth, the wisps of hair at her temples, soothes me.

At the end of the hour, when she gets up to leave, she reminds me, "Many people from Kolabagan are going to come speak about you in the court, you'll see. What a good girl you are, a good student, the only girl in our locality who speaks English. They will learn that you are nothing like what this one newspaper is saying."

I nod, willing no tears to spill from my eyes.

Then the guard calls, "Time, time!" and, after her hand rests for a gentle moment on my head, my mother is gone. I turn back inside. I brace for a collapse, a removal of light during which I will lie, my bones against the floor.

But I am surprised to find that it is bearable. I cook

ruti, I clean the new exhaust pipes which malfunction. Americandi's eyes follow me from task to task, waiting for my breakdown. But it doesn't come. From my mother's immense strength, I have borrowed a little.

JIVAN'S MOTHER
AND FATHER

IN THE DARKNESS OF THE HOUSE, JIVAN'S MOTHER
and father sit before meals of rice and yogurt, tears
falling on their plates.

"It took everything I have," says Jivan's mother, "to
smile before her."

"I know," says Jivan's father, a hand on his wife's
shoulder. "I know. Eat."

JIVAN

ON THE FIRST DAY OF THE TRIAL, UMA MADAM brings me a sari to wear. I recognize it. It is the sari I purchased for my mother from Pantaloons, with my employee discount. It is light blue, the color of a winter day, with simple threadwork along the border. I wear it, and feel my mother close by.

At the courthouse, there is a garden. There is new soil under my feet, the bigness of trees in the yard, light so bright it hits my eyes like broken glass, a stampede of reporters who scream questions and fight to take a picture of my face. Policemen surround me as soon as I exit the van, and I walk as if inside a shell.

Still the reporters shout, "Here! Look here!"

They shout, "What will you say to the families of the dead?"

"What are you eating in the prison?"

"Are they beating you?"

"Has anyone from the terrorist group contacted you?"

"Have they coached you on what to say?"

Inside the courtroom, I sit in relief. The room is large, with ceilings so high they could have fit another floor inside. Long rods drop from the ceiling, holding ceiling fans which turn. Before me, a witness box covered by a white curtain, so that I cannot influence the witnesses.

My lawyer, Gobind, asks me again and again whether I want to eat.

"Want a banana?" he says. "You should eat before it starts."

I have no appetite.

The lawyer for the government begins. He spins a story in which I, unruly local youth, school drop-out, angry at the government, cultivate a relationship with a known terrorist recruiter over Facebook. As proof, the lawyer points to the Facebook conversations I have had with my friend, my foreign friend. In this story, when the recruiter asks for my help, either through coded text messages or by calling me on the phone, I agree. The terrorists need a local contact, the lawyer insists, a helper who can guide them down the unnumbered, crooked lanes of the slum, all the way to the station, and all the way out. In his story, not only do I lead them to the station, I also hurl a torch of my own at the train. I have, he reminds the gathered, hurled bombs at authorities before—

I cannot bear it. I stand up and say, "Those weren't *bombs*, my god, they were just our—"

Gobind hisses at me to sit. The judge, calmly, tells me to sit. Silence thunders in my ears. I lower myself into the wooden chair.

"And," the lawyer concludes, "let me remind the court that all of this is not some, what shall I say, *theory* I have made up. This is all in the confession that the accused signed."

He points at me dramatically.

"Everything I have said," he continues, "is in the confession, and what's more, all of it is corroborated, like I have shown you. The accused herself has repeated many of these statements, as you all saw in her interview in the *Daily Beacon* done by esteemed journalist Purnendu Sarkar."

The judge frowns. He calls both lawyers to his seat, grand like a throne. In my chair, I wait, my limbs growing cold. What is the judge discussing in secret? I feel like a straw doll, dressed up for play, at the mercy of callous children who decide my fate.

Then, mercy. The judge throws out my "confession." He pronounces it inadmissible, as I was forced to sign it—this, he believes.

Gobind gives me an encouraging smile.

I am glad for this small triumph. I have done nothing, I have done nothing, but nobody in this courtroom believes that. Only my mother. My mother is sitting somewhere behind me, but I have no courage to turn around and face all the other eyes.

*

FOR FOUR DAYS, I go through the routine of coming to court. On the fourth day, a reporter, or maybe just a passerby, spits on my face outside the courthouse. My lawyer finds a canteen napkin with which I wipe my face, but there is no time to find a bathroom and wash. I sit with that stranger's hatred on my face all day.

By this time, the prosecution has called forty witnesses, including old neighbors from the slum eviction, the doctor who treated my father, the NGO lady who sponsored my education. They testify behind the white curtain, for fear that I—*I*—may intimidate them by making eye contact. I listen to their ghost voices. Some saw me smoking—several people mention this, as if lighting a cigarette is the same as lighting the tip of a torch.

Is smoking a cigarette as a young woman a crime?

Then, on the fifth day, a man arrives in the witness box. He speaks, and his voice revives me. I know this voice.

I am back in the school courtyard, playing basketball. It is my old PT teacher. I wait for him to tell everyone that I was an ordinary student, that I used to love to play.

He says, "She was poor, always separate from the other girls. But she didn't behave badly in my class. She played very well, in fact. I had high hopes that she would be an athlete."

Listen to my teacher, I think. Listen to him. He knows. I want to catch his eyes to thank him, but it is not possible.

"Yes, my understanding was that she had a difficult life," he says. "Sometimes I gave her food for lunch. I never knew if she had enough to eat. She seemed grateful for the food."

I was, I remember. I was grateful. Perhaps in my child's arrogance I failed to thank him adequately. I will do it as soon as they let me speak to him. I will thank him for speaking up on my behalf. Nobody else has been willing to do it. Not a person from the NGO, not a person from my school, nobody yet from my locality.

Then he says, "But she disappeared. I tried to help her, by being encouraging, by giving her food, but one day she stopped coming to school. This was after the class ten exams. She didn't do so well, if I remember. But so what? You can make up with better marks in class twelve. But no. She just left. Vanished. Never saw her again, until I saw her on TV. Maybe she got involved with criminal elements after leaving school. It happens."

I feel a weight in my chest, the earth's pull within my ribs. I try to hear further, but there are wasps in my ears.

*

FOR THE SIXTH, SEVENTH, and eighth days, my lawyer presents our defense. When I try to persuade him to let me speak, he lifts a finger to his lips.

"Ninety-nine-point-nine percent of the time," he tells me during a break in the proceedings, "it does not help to have the defendant speak. It is a proven fact."

Is it? There is nothing I can do but trust him.

Though I have been in touch with a terrorist recruiter over Facebook, he concedes, all we spoke about was my job, my coworkers, my feelings. Not a word about an attack. I, Jivan, thought he was a friendly boy in a foreign country—what girl wouldn't chat with such a boy?

Gobind points out all the errors in Purnendu Sarkar's article. He corrects the notion that I threw real bombs at the police before. He asserts that my writings on Facebook were nothing more than a young girl expressing her feelings. He paints me as stupid and gullible. And how glad I am for it.

Then he says: "That package that you keep hearing about? That package? Was *not* an explosive of any kind. It was a package of books! She was going to deliver books to a hijra in the slum! That's right, my client was doing public service, she was teaching English to a hijra in her locality. We can hear about it from the hijra herself."

I hear Lovely called to the witness box. My heart lifts, the thread of a kite unspooled, fed into the sky by the hands of a hopeful child.

Lovely has come. The microphone catches her settling into the witness box, and I hear her say, "You are only making these boxes for thin people or what?"

For the first time during the trial, a smile springs to my mouth. Lovely has come, with her voice, her unafraid manner, and the truth of my story.

"What is shocking me," she says in Bengali, "is how you all are making up such lies."

"Please," Gobind tells her, "stick to the facts."

"Fine!" she says. "Jivan was teaching me English. I was not knowing English and *in fact* I am still not knowing English."

The courtroom laughs.

The judge asks for order.

Lovely continues. "But it's not Jivan's fault. Every two–three days, she was coming to my house with some old textbooks. I was learning *a b c d,* then simple words like 'cat.' Like that. I was learning it all so that I was being able to audition better. I am"—she coughs bashfully—"an actress."

The courtroom laughs again.

Lovely continues seriously, as if she has not heard. "I am an actress, so I need to be reading scripts and having fluent English, you understand? So that is how I am knowing Jivan, sweet girl. She was spending her time on teaching the poors. How many of you are doing that in your own life?" she demands. "Who are you all to judge her?"

*

ON THE NINTH DAY, when my one sari is wrinkled, its luster gone, the judge speaks. He clears his throat, and speaks in English. First, he reads out the charges.

Waging of war against the government. Murder and criminal conspiracy. Knowingly facilitating acts preparatory to a terrorist act. Voluntarily harboring terrorists.

"We have given both sides a fair hearing," the judge reads from his prepared notes, his spectacles at the tip of his nose. "The defendant was at the train station, carrying a package. The defendant had an ongoing relationship, on this website called Facebook, with a known terrorist recruiter. The defen-

dant's own former teacher has told us that she left
school, discontinued her education, under suspicious
circumstances. And, on the other hand, we have the
word of a hijra, an individual who begs on the streets
for money, saying the defendant taught her English.
Be that as it may"—the judge takes a deep breath, and
I feel the air in my own lungs—"it is clear that the
defendant has long been disloyal to the values of this
nation. The defendant has spoken clearly against the
government, against the police, on the Internet, on
Facebook dot-com. This lack of loyalty is not something to be taken lightly. It is its own strong piece
of evidence. There is a case to be made, as well, for
soothing the conscience of the city, of the country.
The people demand justice."

He goes on.

They have been unable to trace the terrorists, and
the railway station had no CCTV. Possibly the terrorists crossed the border. They have truly disappeared
into the night. Only I, fool that I am, am here.

Then the judge pauses, and turns the page. The
sound, in the silent room, is like the crack of a whip.
Then the judge sentences the accused to death.

I don't know whom he is speaking about.

Have we moved to a different case?

Somewhere behind me, an animal cries in pain,
as if a bolt has been driven into its brain. It is my
mother. I turn around. My mother, there in the third
row, sari wrapped around her shoulders, stands up,
then collapses. I hear the whole courtroom catch their
breath. My mother falls, and I stand. Two guards

jump up from the back and shout for a stretcher. A huddle of policemen positioned at the exit nearest me watch me like hawks.

When a canvas stretcher appears, the two guards together load her on it—

I shout after them, "Where are you taking her?"

My lawyer tells me to sit down.

"Wait a moment," I shout. "She will get better."

"Please be quiet," calls the judge.

LOVELY

IN THE MORNING, AT THE MUNICIPAL TAP, I AM hearing the news. When I am hearing the chatter about the "murderer," my heart is agitating inside my rib cage.

I was going, just a few days ago, to the court. Even though Arjuni Ma was telling me not to get involved in this court business, I was going. Everybody was thinking that I was being hauled in for something, so proudly I was telling everyone around me, from a Xerox shop lady to a lawyer who was chewing his lips and looking at his phone, that I was there to *give evidence*. That is how Gobind was explaining it to me. The whole time I was wishing for one moment to see Jivan, to be giving her one kind look, but they were putting up white cloths so we were not being able to see each other. One strange detail which they are never showing in movies.

Truly I am not believing this verdict. Surely Gobind will be filing something, appealing something, saving Jivan somehow. Isn't that his job?

I am going to a small crossing by myself and halfheartedly begging for coins. I am knocking at this car and that car. I am seeing a cinema of faces in the windows. In a back seat, a child is squirming. Two men are sitting and drinking Mango Frooti. Even a dog which is looking like a wolf is enjoying the ride in AC comfort. All of them are ignoring me.

The public is wanting blood.

The media is wanting death.

All around me, that is what people are saying. The public is killing her.

When an office worker is walking by, in his clean leather shoes and ironed pants, I am feeling like shouting at him, "People like you killed her! You put your own two hands on her neck!"

Instead I am finding my voice and saying, "Brother, give."

Out of nowhere two child beggars are arriving. They are giving me dirty looks because I am in their territory. They are shouting, "Who made this your crossing?"

I am sticking my tongue out at them and walking away. Behind me I am hearing the two children laughing, shrieking, feeling cursed themselves or maybe just making fun of me.

*

MY FEET ARE TAKING ME to Jivan's house. There are fifty or a hundred reporters there. Their cars and trucks, with satellite dishes on top, are blocking all the lanes. Their cameras and lights and wires are everywhere.

Father of Jivan is leaning on his walking stick, and coming out blinking in the daylight. I am watching from the back of the crowd.

"Look," he is saying, "look at me, I am a lame man, a limp man, and I am not being able to save my daughter."

He is putting his neck forward, like a rooster. "What else are you wanting to know about me?

"Ask," he is saying. "Ask!"

He is looking mad. His arms are trembling. Kalu the neighbor is standing at his side, holding two fingers at the top of his nose, like his eyes are hurting.

"Why you are not asking me anything?" father of Jivan is saying.

The reporters are standing there quietly, for one minute.

Then they are shouting questions. "How do you feel about the ruling?"

"Does your daughter plan to appeal?"

"How is Jivan's mother's health?"

To get his attention they are saying, "Sir! Sir!"

"This way!" they are shouting for a picture.

*

THEN THE REPORTERS are going, leaving behind a trail of crushed cigarettes. At night, I am going out with a broom and sweeping the butts into a corner. The dust is rising at my feet like a little storm.

INTERLUDE

BIMALA PAL'S ASSISTANT
HAS A SIDE HUSTLE

WHO DOES NOT HAVE A SIDE JOB? BIMALA PAL IS GOOD
to me, but even so, I am just an assistant. I have a
family. Wife, school-going children. Have you seen
how much school fees are these days? Besides, when
they come home, tired, they don't want rice and egg
every day. They don't want a tiny TV. We all want
something nice. So I am a middleman, you can say.

Imagine you are a Muslim. One day what happens? Your neighbors, good people, suddenly form a
mob over some rumor and break your door, threaten
your wife, frighten your crippled mother. They set
fire to your house. Thankfully, they do it while you
are all out. That is their kindness. You run. You leave
your damaged house, your property, and you run. Life
becomes so precious, so precious! For a few months,
okay, there is refugee camp, some donated rice, some
tin house.

But one day the government announces, no more

this ugly refugee camp! You all get five lakh rupees, now go somewhere else and live. Shoo.

Immediately, who comes? Vultures.

You have your broker, your landlord, your town council, your water man, your electricity man, even your school man—what will your small children do, sit at home and grow up illiterate like you? So they all come and say, sir, there is a good plot here, you buy and build your own home. Most important you have your own piece of land in your name. There will be a water connection, and electricity cables are already laid, you come and see just. So you look at the plot. The land looks fine. You give most of your compensation money to buy this plot.

Then one day everyone disappears—your broker who called you five times a day? Vanished. The electricity man, the water supply man? Vanished.

Then you go to the address given on your deed and feel confused when you arrive somewhere different from where you went the first time. You have never seen this plot! All the neighborhood boys nod and chew their twigs and nod and then they laugh. When they laugh, you realize—you have bought a patch of this swamp.

So this is the riot economy. In this economy, I am a broker, nothing more.

LOVELY

IN THE MORNING, MY HEART RESTLESS, I AM CALL-
ing the casting director, Mr. Jhunjhunwala. The
phone is still charging, so I am bending my head
close to the plug.

"Hello?" he is saying.

"Hello, me Lovely," I am saying, "good morning
to you!"

Mr. Jhunjhunwala is quiet, only breathing, and I
am feeling his irritation on the line. Now I am realizing, maybe he is always getting such calls from
aspiring actors. Maybe they are not missing any
opportunity to wish him good morning, happy Holi,
good night, blessed Diwali.

So he is sighing and saying, "Yes, Lovely."

"Are you seeing," I am saying, "my demo CD yet?
What are you thinking? Are you having a role for
me?"

"Lovely," he is saying, "please do not call me like
this. I am in a meeting, so, I will call you later, okay?"

"Okay, Mr. Jhunjhunwala, but it has been some
weeks, and you keep saying—"

"I am in a meeting, Lovely," Mr. Jhunjhunwala is saying, and cutting the line.

*

AFTER CLASS ONE SUNDAY, I am asking Mr. Debnath, with some nervousness in my throat, "Are you still keeping me for that role? I was making a demo video, like you were saying—"

He is sitting in his usual chair. He is sighing. I am seeing his belly rise and fall. He is putting his saucer of tea on a side table, and crossing his fingers over his chest. The whole time I am standing before him with my hands crossed behind my back. Mother and father of Mr. Debnath are looking at me from their portraits on the wall. This time their portraits are having some red rose flowers in the garland, as if they are starring in a romance.

"Lovely," he is starting, "do you know how long it can take to make an epic movie like I am making? It can take one and a half years just to cast a film like that. You know in one fight scene I need seventy-two extras? Just one scene. Seventy-two extras. Imagine. Do you think this happens quickly?"

I am hanging my head low like a scolded child.

"On top of that," Mr. Debnath is mumbling, "you have gone and said all these things in court."

"Mr. Debnath," I am saying straightaway, "are you upset with my testimony for Jivan?"

He is staying quiet.

"Don't be silly," he is saying after a while. "Politics is not entering my mind. I am just feeling that, maybe, after the court case, you are already feeling like a big star. Two minutes on TV and, boom, you are thinking you are a legend. You are having so little patience." His thick brows are coming together like worms in the soil. "And the things you said, well, in the papers they are saying you are an unpatriotic . . . I don't want to repeat those things."

"What things?" I am demanding.

I am always thinking that Mr. Debnath is believing in me, but this time, with my eyes on his hairy toes, I am feeling that he is a man I am not truly knowing, and I am a person he is not truly knowing. How long can I keep trusting his words and waiting for his film? My chance to be a young star is reducing. Nobody is wanting to see a star with gray hair and saggy arms.

On the road outside, a blade sharpener is walking by with his tools. He is calling, "Sharpen your knife! Sharpen your knife!"

*

JUST WHEN WE ARE THINKING that the electricity supply is really improved, no load shedding in our locality anymore, it is happening. Suddenly one night the tubelight is going dark. *Kabhi Khushi Kabhie Gham, Sometimes Happiness Sometimes Sorrow,* on the TV is shutting off, leaving some colors playing on the TV screen. It is feeling like something is going wrong with your eyes. But no. It is only load shedding. A few mosquitoes are immediately finding my arms and ears to nibble. Without the noise of fridges and TVs, voices are traveling far in the air.

For once, I am leaving my phone alone, because the battery is finished.

In the dark, with not even a candle in my house, I am sitting in the doorway and looking outside. One hour is passing, then two.

A few people are walking by. I am calling one neighbor lady by name, but it is not her. She is looking at me, a dark face like a silhouette.

Now the sky is holding more light than the ground. There is a half-moon, with gray spots on it that I was never noticing before. Like the moon is having pimples also. Clouds like cotton pulled from a roll are moving under the moon, sometimes hiding it, sometimes revealing it. I am feeling that the world is so big, so full of our dreams and our love stories, and our grief too.

I am blowing my nose and getting up to go inside.

Alone inside, my tears are coming like a fountain. Poor Jivan. My testimony was proving as useful as a shoe is to a snake.

And Azad has not come to see me even once. I am wiping my tears on my dupatta. I was forced to, my heart, is he not knowing that? It was not me who was throwing him out. It was this society. This same society which is now screaming for the blood of innocent Jivan, only because she is a poor Muslim woman.

Like a heartbeat, the light is turning on and the fan is starting to whir and I am hearing a cheer spreading throughout the neighborhood. Electric current is back.

I am wiping my tears. I am flinging my snot outside the window.

When I am thinking about it, I am truly feeling that Jivan and I are both no more than insects. We are no more than grasshoppers whose wings are being plucked. We are no more than lizards whose tails are being pulled. Is anybody believing that she was innocent? Is anybody believing that I can be having some talent?

If I am wanting to be a film star, no casting man or acting coach will be making it happen for me. So I, myself, Lovely with my belly and no-English and dramatic success only in Mr. Debnath's living room—I am having to do it myself. Even if I am only a smashed insect under your shoes, I am struggling to live. I am still living.

When my phone is a little bit charged, I am taking some of my practice videos from acting class, including my super-hit session with Brijesh, and sending them to my sisters on WhatsApp. *Please,* I am writing, *please to be sharing my videos with your friends and their friends. I am looking for acting roles. Tell me if you are hearing about opportunities!*

*

THE NEXT DAY, BACK to my normal life, where I am having to earn money. I am going to the number one tourist spot in the whole city, the white marble British palace Victoria Memorial. It is a place where donkey villagers are coming, especially on cool, cloudy days like these. Their mouths are always open when they are touring the city. They are looking at everything like it was made personally by god. Malls, zebra crossings, women who are wearing pants.

They are also wanting as many blessings as possible, so they are always wearing five holy threads on their wrist and seven holy threads on their upper arm and who knows what else. These poor people are afraid of many things, and top of the list is bad luck from god. This I can understand, however, because me, I am the most cursed person.

Anyhow, I am entering the Victoria gardens and seeing the crowd. There is a straight white path going to the big palace, and on both sides green lawns and trees. In the cool weather, the lawns are full of children who are playing badminton with their parents, and some lovers who are sitting too close together under trees and eating ice-cream cones. They are all taking off their shoes, and I am seeing a parade of cracked soles when I am walking down the center. I am clapping my hands, saying, "Mother goddess sent me to bless you all today."

I am blessing one young girl. Then I am blessing a baby. Then a guard is tapping me with a stick.

"What?" I am saying to the guard. "I am having a ticket, look!"

And the guard is not knowing what to say to that, because that is true. So he is saying, "No walking on the grass!"

Then he is taking a close look at my face. "Aren't

you—didn't you testify at the big trial? Sorry, sorry," he is saying to me, I am not understanding why.

When a man is bringing his baby to me, I am dipping an old flower into my small jar of holy water—water from the municipal pump—and I am circling the baby's head with the flower, dropping dew on the baby, until the baby is looking like he is about to start wailing.

Suddenly a person is saying from behind me, "Lovely, is it you?"

Turning around, I am seeing Mr. Jhunjhunwala. He is wearing jeans and sunglasses which he is pushing on top of his head.

"It *is* you! Ha-ha!" he is saying, like it is such a surprise that I can be roaming in a tourist spot.

I am saying hello, how is your family, and such things.

"Are you free for one minute?" he is saying after a while. "I wanted to—"

I am giving the baby back to the villager, but not wanting to take money for my non-acting trade in front of the casting director. I am saying, "Free blessing for your golden baby!"

Mr. Jhunjhunwala is now face-to-face with me. He is saying, "Look, Lovely, I finally heard about your testimony at the big trial. So I looked at your reel. Your reel is—!" And he is bringing all his fingers together and kissing them.

"My what?" I am saying.

He is continuing, "Then I saw your WhatsApp video. One hundred percent authentic!"

"WhatsApp—"

"The video from your acting classes—"

"My practice videos? From Mr. Debnath's class? How you are seeing it?" I am demanding. "Only my sisters are seeing it." For one moment the mad thought is running in my head—is he coming to laugh in my face? Is he coming to personally tell me that my acting is B-class?

"Are you joking, Lovely?" he is saying. "I think your sisters must be sharing it, because it is all over WhatsApp. My friends forwarded it to me. So many of them forwarded it to me that in the end I was replying to them, 'Okay, okay, I saw it already!' Anyway, now directors are calling me up and saying, 'Is it the same person who gave the most passionate testimony at that trial? Can you book her?' So I think you can be perfect for this music video. Are you available tomorrow?"

*

THE STUDIO IS FULL of stadium-strength lights and silver sheets that people are holding for bouncing the light correctly. I am watching from the side while the two main actors are embracing in front of a green screen.

"Turn, turn, turn," the director is calling. The couple is turning round and round. "Now kiss him on the cheek!"

The actress is looking like she will prefer to kiss an elephant's behind. But she is doing it.

"Cut it," the director is saying.

Then, after some minutes of setup, where they are moving the lights and marking my place on the ground with chalk, it is time for my scene.

My scene is only one. But it is repeating and repeating.

Now the couple is getting married, and I am looking up from blessing the bride and winking at the camera.

I am looking up from blessing the bride and winking at the camera.

I am looking up from blessing the bride and winking at the camera.

I am looking up from blessing the bride and, again, winking at the camera. My eye is twitching. The director is coming up to me in the end, and saying, "Lovely, it is not mattering to me whether your words at that trial are true, false, or in between! All I care about is you have that star material. The nation wants to watch you. You will make this song a hit, I am feeling it!"

*

WHEN A BREAK IS CALLED, I am going searching for some food, and seeing a table full of sponge cakes and fruits. In the heap, I am looking for a picture of a brown cake. I am wanting chocolate flavor. Why not fully enjoy? Finally I am spotting one, at the bottom of the heap, when an assistant is appearing. He is tapping my shoulder with his notepad and saying, "Your break area is over there, outside! This is A-category actors only."

I am still not really understanding this A-category B-category business.

"Okay," I am saying, and turning away.

But the assistant is saying, "Please! You cannot be taking cake from here."

So I am putting it back. I am wishing to ask the assistant if he is not knowing who I am! Is he not seeing my video? But everywhere people are expecting that a person like me will make a scene, so it is my dear wish that I am not making any scene in this professional environment. I am going to join my B-category people, no problem.

Outside the studio, in the field, the light is bright in my eyes. My head is feeling woozy. So long I have been in that studio, where everything outside the circle of lights is black.

There is a crowd of extras around something on a table. A water filter.

A woman is shouting, "How can the water finish? Bring more water!"

I am walking closer and another man is saying, "Let someone faint, then they will learn the lesson."

Other than an empty water filter, there are some blackened bananas on the table. From looking at the bananas I am feeling them in my mouth—squishing on my tongue, smelling a bit fermented, rotting in the heat. So I am swallowing my saliva and waiting for the new water jar to come.

There is another dressed-up woman next to me, so I am tapping her arm and saying, "Sister, which way for toilet?"

The woman is looking me up and down. "What kind of queen are you? Look around, it's all fields and bushes. Go there."

From the woman's voice I am knowing that she is working in the film line for a long time. Her voice is heavy with experience. But how to go to toilet like this, in the bushes, with everybody around? What if the director is coming and I am missing my chance to impress? Worse, what if he is seeing me standing in the field and pissing like a man from under my dress?

I am sighing in frustration and opening Whats-App to tell my sisters what a mess this shoot is. As soon as I am opening WhatsApp, I am seeing there are forty messages. My phone was on silent all this time.

You superstar! one sister is saying to me.

Good job! World is your stage, another sister is saying.

They are all seeing how my video is spreading!

Good theater Lovely. What is this? Even Arjuni Ma has written me a WhatsApp message! Must be she has forgiven me for testifying.

Now I am seeing WhatsApps from people I am not knowing only.

Great acting! they are saying. *Where is this class? So cool!*

*

BACK HOME, I AM slapping the TV to come on, and there I am, on a local news channel, my video with

Brijesh playing on a big screen while some men are sitting in front of it and discussing.

"What is so refreshing about this, Aditya, is seeing these dreamers from all walks of life, gathering to pursue their dream in this authentic way."

I am changing the channel. And there I am again!

"This amateur video of an acting class," one bearded man is saying, "has become a viral sensation in the city. Given the brutal news of the recent days, is it any surprise that the public is hungry for a feel-good take, for a reminder that dreams and dreamers do exist in this city?"

I am pressing the button, and—

"While some people are calling the star of the show, Lovely, a 'terrorist sympathizer,' there are many who insist she is simply standing up for a person she sees as her good-hearted neighbor."

"No doubt," another man is saying, "many are questioning the fairness of Jivan's trial, and Lovely's courtroom performance has a lot to do with it. She is not a legal expert, or an investigator, of course, so it is her *passion* which is getting attention. Stay with us as we will be joined by—"

"What avenues does the ordinary person have to chase their dreams? Tell me, if you don't go to an elite filmmaking academy and hobnob with—"

All these men are lecturing on me! They are having different opinions on whether I am right or foolish, whether Jivan is innocent or evil, but at least they are all discussing me on what they are calling prime-time news!

While I am looking at the screen, somebody is knocking on my door, then peeking in the window and saying, "It's me."

"Arjuni Ma?" I am saying. Immediately I am opening the door, clearing my clothes from the bed, slapping my palms around some over-smart mosquitoes. Inside, she is not sitting. Instead, she is putting her two hands on my cheeks, as if I am a child, and looking at the TV which is still on.

"I am older than you," she is saying to the TV, "isn't it true, Lovely?"

I am looking at her.

"In life," she is saying, "I have learned that we cannot be having everything. For example. To be putting fish on the plate, we are having to sacrifice dignity on the streets. We are having to beg. Why? Because we would be liking to eat. To be left alone by the police, we are having to—well, I don't have to tell you. So this is a moment of sacrifice for you, Lovely. You are on TV. Your video is popular. Don't let that criminal, that terrorist—"

I am opening my mouth to protest, but Arjuni Ma is raising a hand.

"Let her go from your life. You may be fond of that girl, but you must choose: Are you wanting to rise in the film world? Or are you wanting the public to see you as a person who is defending a terrorist? Don't let that case drag you down, Lovely. That is my only advice for you."

"But some people are saying," I am telling Arjuni Ma, "that her trial is not fair—"

"Is that your fight to fight?" Arjuni Ma is saying. "The trial brought you closer to your dream, so aren't you going to reach for what you really want? You want to be a star, or you want to be that girl's defender forever?"

Then she is going, and leaving me alone with the TV. I am muting the volume, which is seeming too high for this small room. On the screen is my practice video. I am watching it silently, feeling something heavy in my stomach which is keeping me sitting on the mattress, keeping my feet stuck to the floor, even though I am wanting to look away. I was never thinking of the question like how Arjuni Ma was putting it, but now I am finding that I am not being able to think of it any other way.

When I am lying down in bed and closing my eyes, I am feeling my heart teaching me its own lesson. My heart is saying: This is who you are, Lovely. You are growing from a family which was betraying you, so this is nothing new. Jivan can be going forward without you also. In fact, this heart is reminding in my chest, you are not even her family. Leave her, this cold box is saying. Weren't you dreaming of being a movie star? Weren't you dreaming of being so close to fame?

This night, I am sleeping in shame, and I am waking in shame, and still shame is weaker than the other thing.

*

SUNDAY MORNING! Time to go to acting class. Fast fast, I am walking down the lane with my hips going like this and like that, past the small bank where the manager was demanding my birth certificate for opening an account. "I was telling him, 'Keep your account,'" I am saying to the camera which is following me. "I was telling him, 'Birth certificate! Am I a princess?'"

The interviewer who is walking beside me is laughing. She is brushing her glossy hair out of her eyes, and saying, "Tell me, how did you start going to this acting class?"

"Well," I am starting. "It was happening like this—"

This time we are together walking past the guava seller in his corner. Usually he is acting like I am invisible, but today he is looking at me with big eyes.

"Here, TV!" he is calling, flapping his hand. "Come take a guava. For free!"

"Brother," I am saying to him, "please to have some dignity. Every other day you are ignoring me, and today you are my best friend?"

The interviewer is laughing again. Many things I am doing are making her laugh. That is fine. Why not to laugh? This TV channel is paying me eighty thousand rupees just for letting them follow me to the acting class. Other TV channels were calling me and offering me money also, but I was choosing this channel because this channel is the most popular. My turn to laugh.

On the train, I am presenting my good profile to the camera.

"A train," I am saying thoughtfully, like a university professor, "is like a film. You see, on the train we can be observing behaviors, arguments, voices. How people are looking happy or upset. How they are speaking with their mother, and with their fellow passengers, and with a pen seller."

The interviewer is looking at me like I am a National Film Award winner. What wisdom is coming out of my mouth! She is nodding and nodding, her eyes shining with the thought of the hundred thousand viewers who will be watching this tonight.

*

IN ACTING CLASS, Mr. Debnath is feeling flustered. Now he is looking like somebody who is never even seeing a camera.

"What is that red light?" he is asking, pointing with a shaking finger at the main camera. "You want me to be looking there?"

"Please just relax, Mr. Debnath," the interviewer is telling him. "You have been teaching this class for years and years. You are the expert. Pretend that we are not even here!"

But that is impossible. Outside the windows of the living room, a crowd is gathering to watch what is going on. "*That* acting class is taking place here!" someone on the street is shouting. One smart fellow is even putting his hand in and moving the curtains so they can all be seeing better.

Inside, the maid is looking suspiciously dressed up, in a shiny sari, with a hibiscus flower in her hair. To the interviewer, she is saying, "Madam, I am watching your show always! And I have been the local cleaner for this class for, oh don't ask me, *years*. I have seen some things. I am available for any show."

While the interviewer is managing her, smiling politely and saying, okay, thank you, Brijesh is coming up to me and mumbling, "Lovely, I am getting"— here he is giggling, hee-hee—"I am getting an offer to do an ad! Detergent ad. They saw me in your video!"

*

THE TV PEOPLE ARE bringing their own overhead lights, making this small living room a land of a thousand suns. Every pimple and scar on my face, you can see, except a professional makeup man put high-quality foundation and concealer. Mr. Debnath's deceased mother and father on the wall, please to pray for them, are looking like their eyes are popping out. Never were they seeing this much glamour in their living days.

For so long I am dreaming of delivering dialogue in front of a real camera, and now I am in front of three! For hours the TV crew are filming us doing practice scenes. In front of them, we are turning up the drama. We are dying patients, supermodels on a runway, mothers cooking food for our husbands. In different scenes, we are having everything from indigestion to love affairs.

In the end, the interviewer is asking me some of my thoughts.

"Society is telling me that I cannot be dreaming this dream," I am telling her. "Society is having no room for people like me"—and inside I am thinking, forgive me, Jivan, I must be leaving you out of this—"because we are poor, and we may not be speaking perfect English. But is that meaning we are not having dreams?"

Now I am confessing, on this show, that many times I was walking in front of the Film and Television Institute, just to see how it was. Just to be a little close to the success of the rich acting students. They were getting casting directors, not just casting agents and coordinators, coming to their classes. They were getting special classes from directors, actors, stuntmen, producers, choreographers.

One crazy day I was even thinking, what if I am giving up this rented room? What if I am just sleeping in the train station and spending my rent money on the big acting school?

I am laughing after I am saying that.

"Ha-ha-ha!" I am laughing. "Can you believe?"

But the interviewer, she is having tears in her eyes. She is putting a hand on my cold hand, like we are newly discovering that we are sisters.

*

FIFTEEN MINUTES AFTER THAT TV segment is playing on cable, this very same night, my WhatsApp is going *prrng!*

I am sitting with my sisters in my room, munching some fried pumpkin snacks, discussing everyone's performance in front of the real cameras. Was Kumar keeping his nervous giggling to a manageable level? Was Peonji impressing with his life story of working in insurance and feeding his three children?

Dear Miss Lovely, my phone screen is saying.

When I am opening the WhatsApp from a number I am not knowing, it is continuing, *I am from Sonali Khan's film production company. Can we talk on the phone?*

I am reading the words again and again. I am showing it, with big, big eyes, to all my sisters. Arjuni Ma, who is acting like she was never giving me any advices, is saying, "Is that—is that—*Sonali Khan?*"

Yes, that Sonali Khan, who is producing one blockbuster after another. Who in this entire country is not knowing the love story, filmed in foreign mountains, in *I Am Yours Forever,* or the fight sequences in the patriotic film *Cricket Mania?*

Suddenly, while we are all sitting there with mouths open, looking at the phone like it is a magic stone, it is ringing. When I am picking up, a woman is saying, "Lovely, did you get my WhatsApp message just now? We are thinking of you for a role in Sonali Khan's next production. It's a good role, a big role. Do you have time to come for an audition next week?"

My sisters are getting excited. They are leaning close to the phone and trying to hear. Everybody is pausing their eating of the pumpkin fritters so that their mouths are not doing *crunch crunch.*

While I am listening on the phone, I am looking with my eyes at my water filter, half-full, my mattress, flattened by our weight, my window, outside of which there is a woman carrying a tub full of soiled dishes for washing.

With all my dignity and all my calm, I, Lovely, am hearing this lady on the phone offering me my dream opportunity. "Yes," I am telling her. "Yes."

PT SIR

IT TAKES TWO WEEKS TO GET AN APPOINTMENT WITH Bimala Pal, and the appointment is no more than the chance to be in a car with her as she is driven from one place to another. The road they travel, in the center of the city, is thick with sedans and buses. A bicycle pushes forward in the wrong direction. Along the edge, tarps are strung between tree trunks for makeshift shops selling calendars, candy, cell phone covers. In the rearview mirror, PT Sir can see two white cars follow.

"Don't ask," says Bimala Pal when PT Sir asks how her work is going. The price of onions is soaring, and this is a problem for the government. She, in the opposition, is getting plenty of mileage from it, at least.

"The public is unsatisfied," she says. "The government is failing to control the price. In the news, if you have seen the reports from local markets, every single person is complaining about the price of vegetables. It is hurting the common person."

Turning to him, she asks if the lane before the school has held up over the months. No more waterlogging?

"None," says PT Sir.

"And this has increased my prestige, in fact," he reveals in a moment of friendly feeling.

At this Bimala Pal laughs.

PT Sir summons all his courage and says what he has wanted to say. "Madam, I want to do more for the party. I am ready for a bigger role. You have so many projects, maybe I can give my service—"

Bimala madam puts a hand on the headrest to brace against a bumpy stretch of road. Through the tinted windows PT Sir sees street-side vendors toss noodles, ladle biryani from giant containers, and scoop the white batter of dosa onto hot griddles. Through the windshield he sees, now and then, without warning, a pedestrian who holds an arm up and dashes across the street. Horns blare, drivers pressing angry palms against the wheel.

After a minute or two of silence, Bimala Pal speaks. "Actually," she says, "good that you bring this up."

PT Sir imagines an office with a leather chair. A computer of his own. An air-conditioned room where he can sit in the evenings, a part-time position to begin with.

But Bimala Pal has something else in mind. He was so good with the teachers in the village of Chalnai, she says, that she would like him to headline a rally at a village where he can present the party's plans for the local school. They need a knowledgeable man like him in the field. And he will get a taste of a politician's life.

"What do you say?"

The balloon pops. Quickly, the vision of a cool and comfortable office evaporates. This will be no different from standing out in the field all day, the blood circulation slowing below his knees. Of course, he accepts.

*

WINTER IS RETREATING, the sun regaining its strength, when PT Sir finds himself in a village called Kokilhat. In the shade of a mango tree with roots like knuckles grasping the earth, PT Sir holds a microphone while two lanky men, sitting on the branches above, support megaphones above his head.

A politician's persona slips easily over his clean white shirt and khakis, the garland of flowers around his neck. PT Sir speaks, recalling notes he studied the day before: "We know that your local school has been closed for over two years! I heard all about the absent teachers, the leaks during the monsoons, the textbooks which were not available. That is why we will renovate the building completely, and hire teachers for every subject. We will make sure discounted textbooks are available before the first day of school for every child. What's more, there will be free midday meals for your children!"

His voice booms from the megaphones. Ducks in a weedy pond nearby flee to the far side.

"Think of this not just as education for your children, but jobs for your family! We will need construction workers, cooks—"

PT Sir feels himself to be a kind of Bimala Pal. He is pleasantly surprised by his confident voice, the feeling of uplift as he stands before a crowd that has grown to a hundred or more. They are mostly men. It is true that many of them are here for the free bags of wheat flour. Still, they are here. PT Sir sees them craning to get a better view of him. He sees them listening to his words. Is this how powerful people feel?

Then a man in the crowd shouts, "Will there be Muslims teaching their religion at this school? Then we will not send our children!"

PT Sir clears his throat. "Well," he begins. "I respect your religion. I respect your sentiment. Public schools are for all, but we will keep in mind your community—"

In the back, where the crowd consists of curious stragglers, some men laugh. A joke drifts through the margins that PT Sir cannot catch.

PT Sir calls, "The important thing is your religion will be respected, your morals will be taught, at this school. I assure you! Vote for Jana Kalyan Party in the upcoming elections!"

PT Sir thumbs off the microphone and hands it to a boy who begins bundling up the cables. The men holding the megaphones throw the metal mouths to a partner waiting below, then leap to the ground, their feet sending up clouds of dust. They clap their palms free of splinters.

It is then that a young man in the middle of the

crowd shouts, "A holy mother cow was *killed*. Yes," he continues, as there is a stunned silence, "killed in our own village!"

People wandering away stop and turn toward him. A small circle opens up around this man, who continues, "What will we do? Will we stand here and listen to a speech about a school? Are we not *men*?"

PT Sir raises his arms. "Be calm, brother," he calls. "Better that you don't spread rumors."

But the crowd begins to agitate. Men shout, "Who was it? Who was it?"

"Who killed the cow?"

"Whose cow?"

From where he stands, PT Sir shouts, "Please be calm, your village chief will investigate—"

Nobody is listening to him. PT Sir hears names floating, names of the only ones who eat beef.

PT Sir shouts again, "Rain is coming, please be calm and—"

But the crowd bellows and lumbers, like a many-limbed animal discovering its ferocity. As one they direct their feet to the area where the Muslim villagers live.

PT Sir follows the crowd. Only a few minutes ago he was in full control of these men, inspiring them with words about school. Now they speed down narrow and narrower lanes, passing by children who look up from bathing, their eyes peering out from soaped faces. Mothers and fathers appear and snatch up the children, drawing them inside despite their cries.

"Stop," PT Sir cries. "Listen here! The party will not be happy with you all. Don't you want the school—"

Unbelieving, his heart beating too fast, beside him the impassive face of the driver who drove him here, PT Sir watches the crowd find the house. He watches them rattle the chain on the doors, then break the flimsy panels open.

INTERLUDE

THE VILLAGERS VISIT THE BEEF-EATER

KILL HIM BECAUSE HE ATE BEEF, THAT MUSLIM.

Come prepared with daggers and homemade pistols, and we will go as a force of the good god to that man's house. His door surprises us—two rotting planks of wood held together by a chain which, when we grip it, leaves our fingers smelling of iron.

But no, it is not that which surprises us, but the fact that we remember gripping this chain to rattle, innocent. "Brother, borrow your ladder?" we asked him before.

You see, he is our neighbor. A decent man, sure. His beard descends as a cloud to his chest, and our sons fear him for how he tests their mathematics whenever he sees them. "Eight times five?" he says to them. "Square root of forty-nine?"

They say he used to be a schoolteacher, but of what use is that? We all used to be something else.

Now, behind the door we know well, the stillness of the house strikes us as false. It makes us angry.

The heat of the day, our empty stomachs—we are not happy. How could we be happy when our sacred mother cow is being senselessly slaughtered? Do not forget! The cow who has given us milk (oh yes), and has drawn the plow through our great-grandparents' fields (yes), and has borne our goddess to her heavenly home (oh yes), that very cow has been killed like a common pest by this Muslim. What can we do? What must we do?

In the room behind the door, three daughters, too young to be of any use. We cut them like their father cut our holy mother cow. Our people, the true people of this nation, are a flood of cleansing water, our arms and legs full of muscles which grab and swing, our grip never more certain than when it closes around the resistant throat of the man's wife. Never more certain than when it stretches open her legs.

—Too ugly! we think at first.

—Aha, not too ugly after all, we know later.

We shatter the fading photographs on the wall, we shake the cupboard until a few gold bangles fall out, and we fall upon the gold like it is a drop of water in a desert.

Rolled up in the corner, a carpet for praying on, so we piss on it, and laugh. A terrified man is dragged down from the roof, the Muslim we are after. He moves his mouth, but he has taken out his dentures, and his sunken cheeks beg and beg before his voice finds itself. He joins his hands in prayer, and we say, "Now you have learned to pray properly?"

He watches his wife's legs opened by the true men

of this country, and he appears to die before we can kill him.

Anyway, we stomp on his skull so that the cream of his brain splatters on the floor. Teach him to have ideas about killing our holy mother cow, whom we love and respect.

Later my man says, opening the small icebox and hauling out a chicken, "But where is the beef?"

PT SIR

PT SIR LIES IN BED THAT NIGHT, AN ARM FLUNG OVER his head, his wife snoring by his side. He looks at the shadows cast on the ceiling by passing headlights, and in a kind of daze he knows this much: His career in politics is over. Never before has he thought of it in such grand terms—"career in politics"—but now, on the verge of losing it, he knows how close he has come to having it.

What did he witness today? With each turn of the ceiling fan's blades, he knows, and he refuses to know. He pulls a blanket up to his chin, and covers his ears in the warm cloth. He knows what he watched, and in watching and not lifting a finger, condoned. He is no less than a murderer. He turns from side to side, seeking a position of comfort, until his wife drowsily scolds him. Then he lies on his back, still as a corpse.

In the morning, eyes gritty with sleep, he cannot stand to shave his face. He cannot bear to look at his face in the mirror. What face is this? Does it belong to him? He prepares to tell Bimala Pal what happened, and to offer his resignation from the party roll. Perhaps her benevolence will keep him out of jail, perhaps it will not. The massacre happened in his presence, perhaps even started from his comments about religion.

The sun rises higher in the sky and, somehow, absent from his body, PT Sir finds that he has bathed himself and eaten a simple breakfast of oats. He has worn his shirt, and tied his shoelaces, and now he stands at the door, ready to go.

*

WHEN PT SIR APPEARS at her door, Bimala Pal is pacing in the living room, a phone held at her ear. She wears a beige shawl whose frilly edge flaps as she walks. She gestures at him to sit, and disappears into the office.

PT Sir sits at the edge of the sofa. He feels faint, and lowers his head between his knees. A concerned assistant offers him cold water, and he gulps down one glass, then another.

When Bimala Pal emerges, she asks, "How was your rally?"

Then, looking at his sweating face, she says, "Are you feeling all right? Do you need water?"

PT Sir shakes his head.

"I had water," he replies, the words catching in his dry mouth. A high-pitched keening lingers in his ears. Following her to her office, he feels that his legs have disappeared.

"Actually," he begins, once they are in the closed office. "The rally yesterday . . ."

"You don't look well," observes Bimala Pal. "I'll tell Raju to call a taxi for you—"

"No," he interrupts. He cannot leave now. "One thing happened at the village."

PT Sir tells Bimala Pal everything. His tongue forms its own words, and he barely hears them over the drumbeat of his pulse. When he finishes, the two of them sit in silence. A crow alights outside the window and harshly caws. Through the closed glass of the window, PT Sir can see its outline.

For a while, Bimala Pal looks silently at the crow too.

PT Sir waits for her to tell him to leave, to never contact the party again. He will return to his schoolteacher's life. It was what he had, before. It was not unbearable.

Then she looks up and gives him a smile. "Have a biscuit," she says, pushing an open packet toward him. "You know, it is sad that a man died, very sad about the children too. I can see you are disturbed. I understand. But did you lay a finger on them? Did you personally hurt them in any way?"

When PT Sir realizes that she is waiting for his reply, he shakes his head.

"Then why," Bimala Pal says, "are you taking the weight of it on your own shoulders?"

PT Sir comprehends each word a moment after she speaks it. Could she be forgiving him?

"There is nothing to forgive," says Bimala Pal. "In politics, you will see, sometimes it feels that you are in charge of everything and everyone. But we can only guide them, inspire them. At the end of the day, are they our puppets? No. So what can we do if they raise their hand, if they decide to beat someone, if they feel angry?"

PT Sir dislikes this justification. At the same time, he reaches desperately for the only relief he has felt since the massacre. Bimala Pal does not seem angry. She does not even seem surprised.

Looking at Bimala Pal's good-natured face, her hands joined on the table in front, her kind eyes wrinkled at their corners, PT Sir feels that she has saved him. From what, he no longer wants to imagine. Yes, she has saved him.

When Bimala Pal speaks next, he understands that she has known what happened all along.

If anybody asks, she tells him, PT Sir is to say that the unstable brick house in which the man was living collapsed. It spontaneously collapsed. And how does PT Sir know? He was doing a rally nearby. It is true that the house did collapse—when the party wrecked it with hammer and ax. It is true that the house did fall upon a man who died.

All of that is true, Bimala Pal reminds him, a gentle smile on her face.

Afterward, PT Sir walks down the road, feeling the protective wing of the party sheltering him. He opens his mouth and gulps air until a beggar looks at him strangely. The Muslim man's family perished, nobody is denying that, but he himself will be all right. Maybe that is all that can be salvaged.

At home, when he parks himself in front of the

TV—he has taken a sick day from school—his mind wanders while his eyes remain captive. When late afternoon comes, with its hint of darkening, he surrenders to heavy sleep which anchors him to his bed till he is running late for school the next morning.

For days, the matter eats away at him. His wife asks, meanly, "Have you fallen in love with a teacher at your school or what? Your head is somewhere else these days."

How he wants to tell her. One night, he climbs into bed beside her and smooths the rolled cotton inside the blanket cover for something to do with his hands. After a long while he says, "Are you listening?"

His wife, watching a recipe video on her phone, jumps, and laughs. "I was so absorbed in this pasta, four different kinds of cheese, look, I forgot you were—"

PT Sir makes such an effort to put together a smile. He does. But he cannot knit one together.

"Who died?" she teases. "That teacher you are always dreaming of?"

PT Sir looks down into his lap then. If he looks her in the eye he may cry. A grown man.

"Something has happened," he says. "It's bad."

This gets his wife's full attention. She casts her phone to the side of the pillow.

When she holds his hands in her own, he begins to speak. He tells her everything.

JIVAN

AFTER THE COURT'S RULING, THE PRISON NEWLY encloses me, the walls more solid than they used to be. Americandi watches me return to my mat. She watches me take off the blue sari, my mother's sari, memory of its gifting removed from it. She watches me lie down, a storm in my mind so dark it pulls all light from my eyes. She chews popcorn with her mouth open, and spits unpopped kernels in the corner, which I will later clean.

Then a skinny young woman appears and begins giving Americandi a foot massage, wrapping her soft arms around the smelly soles, calling her aunty. I have not seen this woman before. She is new. I watch from my mat, the weave of straw pressing itself into my knees and palms. My mind screams and quiets itself, screams and quiets itself.

Americandi leans back on her mattress, resting her neck on the wall. She asks no questions. She knows already, or she does not care.

She closes her eyes and says, "Ah, yes," and the new prisoner sways with her whole body in the task.

*

"YOU COME WITH ME NOW," Uma madam says one day, after breakfast. She has come prepared. A male guard comes forward and grabs my arm.

"Where?" I say, wrenching free. He lets go. "Stop it! I need to talk to Gobind about the appeals."

"You walk or he will drag you," says Uma madam in reply.

Back in my cell, I gather my sleeping mat, my other salwar kameez, slip my feet into the rubber slippers, then look around for anything else that is mine. Nothing is.

Uma madam pulls my dupatta off my neck. When I grab at it, she clicks her tongue.

"What use is modesty for you anymore?" she says.

We walk down the corridor, the three of us, and a few women look up from inside their cells. The corridor is so dim they are no more than movement, shapes, smells, a belch. Perhaps sensing my fear, Uma madam finds it in her heart to explain. "You can't have a dupatta in this place where you are going. Not allowed. What if you decide to hang yourself, what then? It has happened before." After a pause, she says, "Nobody's coming to see you, don't worry about looking nice."

Uma madam unlocks a door at the far end of the corridor, which opens onto a staircase I have never seen. Though the day is dry and sunny, there is a puddle of water on the top step.

"Go down," she says.

When I don't move, she insists, "Go! Don't look so afraid, we don't keep tigers down there."

I climb down, my slippers slapping the steps. When I touch the wall, it is cold and damp. On the floor below, there is another corridor, a shadow of the one above. This corridor looks like nobody has set foot in it for months. A bat flaps around, panicked, near the ceiling. It doesn't know how to get out of this place.

Uma madam looks upward, her eyes too slow for the winged rat. "This is the problem," she says to the male guard, who follows us, "do you see? I told them keep her upstairs, otherwise I have to go up and down, up and down. Can my knees take it, at this age?"

The guard looks at his feet and gives a dry laugh. I can tell he is laughing not at her knees but at something else.

Then Uma madam unlocks a barred room. The guard, who has hovered behind my shoulder all this while, steps back.

Here it is, a special cell for the soon to be dead. A room under the ground for the ones who will be soil.

*

BUT THEY CANNOT KILL me before they kill me.

Since my ruling was handed down by the highest court, I have only a mercy petition left. For this too I need Gobind's help. There is no time for me to study the law books myself.

Some days, however, it feels like time is all I have.

It is cool here, where the sun never comes, even on the hottest days. I crouch on my mat, arms naked and cold like a plucked chicken. In one corner, a low wall separates the room from the toilet, which is a hole in the ground from which dark cockroaches emerge, their whiskers feeling. The first time I see one, I whack it with my slipper.

Now I flick one and another away with my fingers. It is a game of carrom. More fun when the carrom disks, tossed into the drain, come back for another round.

Night begins early, and has no end. When I am certain the sun will never show its face again, I lie down on the mat, and will myself to dream of a tunnel, scraped with nothing more than my fingernails, a tunnel which sets me loose in a village far from here.

PT SIR

WEEKS LATER, IN AN ELECTRONICS SHOP, AN EMPLOYEE with a lanyard around his collar sets a large box on the ground. PT Sir and his wife look expectantly at the box. Around them, a wall of televisions plays a football game. In the next section, customers stand thoughtfully before rows of refrigerators. PT Sir's wife has marveled at the fridges with two doors, the fridges which can create and deposit ice cubes, the fridges which have sensors which tell you when the door is left open.

"Technology," PT Sir has told her, "keeps moving forward."

"Demand for tandoor is a bit low," explains the salesman now. "It is such a specialized oven, for serious chefs. So we stock only one brand, the top brand."

PT Sir's wife looks at the box, and smiles, her teeth bright on her face, her hands playing with the thin end of her oiled plait, like a child.

"It has an aluminum tray and toughened front glass window," continues the employee, a young man, removing the foam and plastic from the box.

"Fully modern look. Right now there is a special offer where you get kebab skewers free with this! And best of all, efficient electricity consumption, sir, your bill won't increase at all!"

With the packaging removed, what sits on the ground is a low black cube.

"Madam," the salesman continues, holding the lanyard to his chest with one hand, "I will tell you the best advantage of this brand is—it cooks fast! If you try to make a chicken kebab in the oven, it may take almost an hour. But here, it is done in fifteen to twenty minutes. And completely authentic clay-oven taste!"

"Hmm," says PT Sir's wife. "What about pizza?"

"Pizza like foreign, madam, you will think you are in London—"

"That is all okay," interrupts PT Sir, "but tell us the real information. How much is it?"

The employee laughs. "Sir, once you eat the five-star food from this tandoor, you will see it's *saving* you money. Your favorite restaurant is at home!"

PT Sir waits. His wife waits. Somewhere, in a section they can't see, a salesperson demonstrates the capacity of a speaker, and a deep bass booms in their ribs.

"Okay," the employee begins, pulling out a calculator, "let's see. This model comes to five thousand seven hundred rupees."

"Why that much?" says PT Sir. "We were looking at other models on the online shops, maximum four thousand."

"Online shops," says the employee, "will ship you a bad part, or a defective secondhand machine. The stories we hear from customers, you don't want to know. Here you have a three-year warranty. My name is Anant, sir, call me anytime, I work here six days a week."

PT Sir's wife turns to him. "This is a good brand," she whispers. "Top of the line. They use it on TV also. Don't be stingy."

The employee stands respectfully at a distance, and looks at his phone.

"If we're buying," says PT Sir's wife, "we should buy the best. Especially now you are earning *double* income . . ." She smiles.

"Not *double*," protests PT Sir.

"Almost double. Isn't the party giving you—"

"Shh!" says PT Sir. A flake of anger catches on his tongue. He swallows. His mouth is too dry, and then—he can feel saliva filling his mouth, as it did while he watched the beef-eater murdered. Not a person knows—other than his wife, and Bimala Pal, and a few trusted party men.

"Be calm," his wife says. "So much tension is not good for your health. Anyway, you're a true party man now. Isn't this what you wanted? Aren't you proud?"

He notes in her words both reward and punishment. But she touches his arm gently, and her presence soothes him. They buy the tandoor. Paying for the tandoor in a sheaf of cash, he feels rich. He feels powerful in how casually he decides that he will buy it, that he will pay the full amount right away.

Monthly installments are for the common man. He? He has ascended.

*

REWARDED FOR HIS LOYALTY, now with a salary from the party, PT Sir spends evenings and weekends traveling to districts across the state, doing events for teachers, students, and parents. In Shojarugram, he sees banners with his face on it and, in Bengali, *Welcome to the headmaster of our village!*

"I got a promotion," he jokes with the driver.

The driver gives him a smile in the rearview mirror. "To the rural people, your visit is the biggest event of this month, maybe!"

At each school, students sweep the soil courtyard with brooms. Saplings, newly planted, grow within the protection of twig fences. PT Sir is jostled as he joins his hands in greeting before pushing through the crowd to enter the school building. Everywhere he goes, the scene is the same. About fifty teachers and parents are crammed into the building, and dozens more wait outside. They are usually silent. This is how the events start, he knows now. They will find their voice by the end, when he has become less of a deity and more of a man, sometimes with a cough caused by the dust of the villages.

"Jana Kalyan Party is starting," he says into a loudspeaker which echoes, "scholarship programs for girl children. In the coming election remember to cast your vote for Bimala Pal and Jana Kalyan Party."

At one school, when the electricity cuts out, a loud

generator powers a portable light. Winged insects buzz and knock. A tiny toad comes hopping into the school building, and a schoolboy is made to pick up the creature and set it loose outside.

After the speech, the gathered share grievances with PT Sir. A group of gap-toothed mothers and frowning fathers complain: Teachers don't bother to come to school. Of what use is a scholarship, and of what use a school building, if there are no teachers?

The teachers, in turn, tobacco tucked in their mouths, protest that they are not paid their salaries on time. Their monthly salary comes two months later, sometimes three. How are they supposed to feed their families?

The younger teachers argue: What about progress or raises for them? They find it a dead-end job.

"It is your work to build the nation's future!" says PT Sir. "Isn't that noble?"

When the moment of departure is near, no matter how fervently they had been complaining and protesting, the teachers clap for him, a cheerful din that PT Sir absorbs with a smile. What are they clapping for? He doesn't know, but he is used to it. The people clamoring to see him, to hear his words, the grandmothers holding his hands, the garlands and praise, the prayers, all directed to him, as if he is a god. Who wouldn't find something electric in it?

*

THE NEXT EVENING, there is an important meeting at Bimala Pal's house. As PT Sir sets off, his wife admires his traditional clothing, his shined shoes. "You are starting to look like a politician!" she says.

"Is that so?" he says.

This pleases PT Sir, though it is a meager reward. For what has he spent his days falsifying the truth in court? For what has he taken on the ghost of the beef-eater, that man who begs for mercy in the moments before sleep? That ghost who weeps in his mind when he is alone, who pleads with him when he waits for the schoolgirls to come to the field?

*

AS THE STATE ELECTIONS approach, the party steps up its campaign to recapture the state legislative house. So long they have been the opposition. Here is their opportunity to form the next government.

At this meeting, Bimala Pal wishes to hear what their platform on education might be. From the past months of engaging with the teachers and parents among their constituents, what have they learned?

PT Sir clears his throat. Suddenly, he is thankful for all the field visits. "Bring another tea," whispers someone at the far end to the tea boy, who is hovering. Who knows what the boy makes of all this? Who knows if he goes to school?

In the silence of the party's gaze upon him, PT Sir recognizes all those teachers' complaints for the treasure chest they are. He has laid his ear to the ground, and heard the unmediated voice of the public. There is no greater currency in this room at the moment. PT Sir tells the room, with casual gravity, what he has heard. Then he proposes, "The greatest issue in education around the state does not have to do with syllabi or supplies. It has to do with personnel. It is the personnel who are voting, not the books."

At this some of the older men at the table chuckle. Historically, education strategy has focused on syllabi—altering syllabi to tell the histories that serve the ruling party.

"Forget syllabi," PT Sir continues. "First of all, teachers' salaries need to be paid within the first three days of the month, without fail. This is the single biggest complaint I have heard. Teachers don't want to do their jobs because they're not getting paid on time. So they don't show up to school. Then the students stop going. This is one change, a concrete change, we can make and talk about. I think it will bring the teachers' votes to us."

Bimala Pal listens. She has on her mind not only schools but floods in the north of the state, ruined crops and stranded villagers. She has on her mind new trains connecting the state to the capital, safety in the mines, quotas for different castes and tribes. She has on her mind beautification of the city, planting of flowers by the roads and regular watering of trees in public parks. The city voters cannot be neglected. There will be a function the next day where she awards laptop computers to high-achieving students of the city.

"That may work," an older man says, now looking at PT Sir. "Madan is eating everyone's head about the syllabus. So this is a fresh approach."

Madan Choudhury, the current education minister, is behind the state's push to include more patriotic texts in school syllabi.

"To be honest, I see his point of view," interrupts another man. "Who is this Hemingway? Who is Steinbeck? Madan is pushing to have more original Bengali literature, and we have to continue that push."

PT Sir feels that he is vibrating with energy. Let the old-timers try to challenge him. Just let them. Hasn't he been a teacher? Doesn't he know what life in the school is really like? He knows, more than these career bureaucrats who have not seen the inside of a school since 1962!

He continues, "With all respect, we have to take care of the people before taking care of the ideology. Through people is how we will spread ideology, not by neglecting them."

Some raise their eyebrows in appreciation. Bimala Pal looks at PT Sir with a hint of a smile.

"You turned out," she says, "to be quite a persuasive orator!"

"He's a teacher after all," says someone else. "How can he *not* have a commanding side?"

On the train, PT Sir holds his head high. Near his house, he gives a five-rupee coin to a beggar child who sits on the pavement, looking up with blank eyes.

How did it happen? His colleagues at the school, those teachers, those ladies, with their cinema gossip and recipe trades, their husbands and children to return to—their lives continue as they always have, above the watermark of political tides. But in the villages, those other teachers look at him with hope and desperation. They look at him as somebody who can do something. So, he thinks, perhaps he can.

*

IT IS SUMMER, ROADSIDE trees dry and dusty, when PT Sir hands his resignation letter to the principal. She tears it open, glances at it, and jokes, "Now you are a powerful man, what use do you have for our humble school?"

PT Sir presses his teeth on his tongue in a show of humility.

Then, his three-week notice dismissed by the principal, having declined the offers of a farewell party, pleading to be excused for the busy electoral campaign, PT Sir is free. PT Sir is no longer a PT Sir. At this thought he feels mournful. The defiant and silly girls were children, after all. Walking down the lane, he looks back at the building one more time. In the barred windows, ponytailed heads appear. He feels a tug of nostalgia for his old life, and then, in a moment, it is gone.

*

THE FOLLOWING DAY, WHEN PT Sir visits Bimala Pal's house, the living room is a tangle of cables and chargers, young men and women on every available seat, their faces lit in the blue glow of screens. PT Sir notes, impressed, that this is the campaign's social media team.

At an office elsewhere in the city, a video production company releases short films on YouTube every week, highlighting the lives of ordinary people positively affected by the initiatives of the party. These films are played on LED billboards at intersections, and on mobile screens carried by small trucks through villages. On Facebook, the films gather tens of thousands of views.

PT Sir's work is on the ground. Every day, he is driven in a party Sumo car to towns and villages across the state. When he covers all of the nineteen districts, he starts over again. His car speeds past vegetable markets under tarp, past green hills and rocky outcrops, past streams which run dry, their sandy bottoms exposed. He smiles at curious men who tap on the car's tinted windows, and steps out and greets village elders who sit on porches, their faces wrinkled from decades in the sun. He wags his finger and delivers speeches under welcome banners strung between the limbs of trees.

He meets with teachers and teachers' unions. He drinks endless cups of tea. He smiles until his cheeks ache.

"Until I gave up my job to represent you all," he begins every speech, "I was a teacher, like you!"

Now and then PT Sir looks, from the stage, for a glint of a knife, or a weapon held high in the air.

*

FROM THE YOUNG MEN and women working on social media, phones attached to their palms at all times,

Bimala Pal learns about the angry Twitter and Facebook messages. They arrive, blips and bloops on lap-
tops and phones, bubbles and boxes of typo-riddled,
emoji-filled complaint.

*Y is Jivan getting a shot at a mercy petition? Mercy
4 wut??*

*Justice now!!! Dont forget the 100+ innocents who
died!!!*

*This case will drag on for a decade and use up our tax
money, nothing else will happen.*

*Why r we payin 4 that terrorist 2 sleep and eat and
relax in prison while some mercy petition goes thru the
system? If u become the govt how will u handle?*

It doesn't end.

*

ON ELECTION DAY, a statewide holiday, PT Sir wakes
up at four in the morning. A peculiar exhaustion
slows his body, the exhaustion of getting up in darkness, and turning artificial lights on. His limbs are
slow. While the sky lightens, he bathes, a stream of
cold water falling down his back to the bathroom
floor.

Soon, a car arrives to take PT Sir to cast his vote.
His polling station, which is Bimala Pal's too, is a
local school, closed for the day. Where on other days
children fill water from coolers, where they linger
and play and drop crumbs of lunch, there are now a
dozen TV cameras and trucks carrying generators.
Reporters drink paper cups of Nescafé purchased
from a vendor who makes rounds with a kettle. Above

them, barred windows conceal silent classrooms, their desks scratched in teenage love and impatience.

Already there is a long line of voters. A house-wife with sequined slippers, a maid with a thin shawl thrown over her sari, a man with alcohol-red eyes. A woman feeds a stray dog a biscuit, and the people behind her idly watch.

As soon as Bimala Pal and PT Sir emerge from their sober white Ambassador car, the reporters rush to them, jostling to position a microphone or a small recorder before them. Beside Bimala Pal, PT Sir joins his hands in greeting, and bows his head. In the great humility of this gesture he feels a shiver of electricity run through him. How close to power he is. He will be on every television screen in the state, and that is the least of it.

Inside the school building, in an assembly hall, Bimala Pal, like every other voter, casts her vote at a machine situated on a curtained desk. When she emerges, she receives an indelible ink dab on her index finger, at the border of fingernail and skin.

*

THE NEXT DAY, NEARING the hour when election results will be declared, Bimala Pal's house bursts with people—politicians, clerks, assistants, union leaders, even a stray celebrity or two. A TV plays on high volume in the corner, and shouted conversations are carried on over it. Somebody comes through the door carrying a sack of kochuri, fried bread, and a tub of alur dom, potato curry.

Then a phone call comes, and the room falls silent. Bimala Pal disappears into the office, the phone held at her ear.

"Where's the remote?" someone yells. "Turn this TV down."

PT Sir paces, smiling tightly at the others gathered. In his mind, a racetrack of worries: What if the party doesn't win? What if he gave up his job prematurely? An older man calls to him, "Be calm. Don't take so much tension, not good for your young heart."

He continues, "It hasn't been six months that I've had a pacemaker." He points to a spot below his left collarbone.

"I'm not worrying," lies PT Sir. "Why don't you sit, sir, let me find a chair . . ."

When Bimala Pal emerges from her office, she holds the receiver at her side, a sly smile on her face. Men in front break into shouts, and a whoop of triumph lifts the room. Bimala Pal laughs as men around her, her assistants, playfully raise her arms in theirs, like she is a boxing champion.

"Did we win?" PT Sir asks, unbelieving. "Did they call it?"

Jana Kalyan Party has won the majority of seats in the legislative assembly. Bimala Pal, as the leader of the party, is now chief minister of the state.

"Get ready," says the man with the pacemaker, "for the real work to begin."

PT Sir nods gravely, as if he understands what is to come.

Boxes of sweets promptly appear, and are passed from hand to hand. Somebody sends sweets out to the reporters swarming the lane, and a din rises from the gathered men and women of the media. Soon they make way for visitors arriving to congratulate the party. A rival party chief graciously brings an enormous bouquet, and the scent of roses fills the room. A renowned football player arrives, and a cricket player too. Musicians arrive, and film stars in sunglasses. A garland is draped about Bimala Pal's neck, then another, and another, petals drifting down to the floor, pausing now and then in the folds of her sari.

PT Sir watches the hoopla and eats a sweet, grinning from ear to ear. He shakes hands when hands are offered, and claps backs when he is embraced. The vitality of the moment dazes him. Never has he been in a place that felt so much like the center of the world.

When he looks for an empty surface on which he can sit, he notes how the room has filled up with bouquets and garlands, dewy petals duly misted by an assistant who carries a water bottle with him, looking harassed. Through the windows, he sees the crowd outside grow bigger and noisier, a collection not only of cameramen but of well-known reporters, bigger television crews, neighborhood fans, even one comedian. They chant and cheer. Snacks that are brought to Bimala Pal are frequently distributed among those waiting outside. PT Sir watches them, those common people who will always be on the outside.

*

LATE IN THE AFTERNOON, the chief minister–in–waiting beckons PT Sir to join her in her small office. She closes the door behind them.

Inside, banners rolled into tubes lean in the corners, and old desktop computers sit on the floor. Though Bimala Pal's seat is a luxurious leather chair, a towel draped on it for protection and cleanliness, the new chief minister does not sit. She stands before the dark wood desk.

"What do you think," she says, "about a senior secretary post? In the education ministry, of course. It will be good for you."

PT Sir forces himself not to grin. He must look like a serious man. In this room, with the tubelight casting a sad glow on the large table, the idols of gods arrayed in a nook in the wall, the scent of incense curling upward from sticks, his life is transformed. It is the kind of room which, at night, attracts the attention of flying insects and house lizards.

"The teachers," PT Sir says instead, "they delivered, didn't they? Our work with them was good."

This much he has learned: A successful person is a magnet for resentment. Deflecting the light of success away from him is a better practice. But Bimala Pal will not accept it.

"*Your* work with them," she says. "Don't be humble. You can't be humble in politics."

PT Sir smiles.

"How does it feel?" she asks.

"I am ready to serve," he replies. "I will gladly accept that post you are thinking about."

He turns to leave, his body buoyant with relief. Outside, he will glide past the men drunk on syrup from sweets, their heads big with knowledge of their new importance. He will glide past the assistants and interns, the social media youths, no longer required to remember their names. At home, no doubt over a celebratory meal, he will tell his wife. He relishes it. He is about to turn the doorknob when Bimala Pal speaks.

"One thing," she says. "Jivan, that terrorist. She has been polling high on voters' priorities."

"Oh," says PT Sir, taken aback by the turn in the conversation. He should have known.

"This issue is not going away." Bimala Pal touches her forehead in a gesture of worry. "Something will have to be done. The public is unhappy that she is appealing for mercy and whatnot."

"I testified—"

"That is why I am telling you," Bimala Pal interrupts.

"And the mercy petition is her legal right, so I don't know—"

"Legal right? You have much to learn about politics," says Bimala Pal, smiling.

Then her smile fades, and she looks at him, unblinking, until PT Sir feels his relief vanish.

It is clear what he has to do. He draws a breath to speak, keen to crack the tension in the room. "Isn't it always the quiet ones who turn out to have dangerous thoughts in their head?"

"That may be so," says Bimala Pal. "Listen, this is a result we can deliver as soon as we take power. It will be a big victory for us."

PT Sir knows that if the terrorist is—well, if the matter of the terrorist is *resolved* during their tenure, this government's approval from the public will know no limits. They will have bought themselves time to implement other campaign promises.

"The mercy petition is all that stands in the way," says Bimala Pal. "See what you can do about it? The court gave its verdict. The people want justice. Anyway"—she smiles—"you will know best. Your student, after all."

LOVELY

DAY OF THE AUDITION! ON THE ROAD, MY SLIPPERS are going *flap flap*, and I am praying, please slippers please not to tear today. I have tied my petticoat too low and my belly is jiggling, but no time to fix that. The guava seller is there again. For fun I am asking him the time.

"Were you showing my guava on your TV interview?" he is grumbling. "Why I am telling you the time, then?"

I am laughing and waving my hand. I am knowing what the time is, because I am planning my whole morning so I can be taking the eight fifteen local train to Tollygunge.

"This is a ladies' compartment," one aunty is yelling, "can't see or what?"

"Move, madam," I am replying respectfully. "I am just going to the other compartment."

"Oh!" she is saying after she is seeing my face. "Aren't you—I saw you on—"

I am squeezing past her.

In Tollygunge, I am walking under a row of trees.

Under one tree, a man is ironing clothes with a coal-loaded frame. Under another tree, a sweeper is sweeping plastic from the gutter. Then I am seeing a villa, surrounded by a clean white wall over which pink flowers are spilling.

Outside the gate, sitting on a plastic chair, there is a man. He is thin like a grasshopper, and his freshly cut hair is standing straight up on his head. He is looking at me coming closer and closer, and he is saying, "Please, ma, not today, there is an audition going on—"

"Very strange you are!" I am telling him right away. "I am coming for the audition only!"

To this the man is not knowing what to say. He is looking like his boss is going to fire him, but he is not knowing how to stop me. I am looking that good. I am feeling that confident. So what if some man is trying to put a barrier in front of me?

Inside, there is a big white building, surrounded by a tidy garden. So many flower beds, and so many nice benches. They are all empty because people are preferring the cool weather of AC.

So I am pushing open the big wooden door, and feeling the air on my skin. Inside, there is a big room with colorful sofas, on which people with stylish hair are sitting. Their perfumes are mingling and my nose is enjoying. Behind glass partitions there are other people working. Some framed film posters are on the walls. The reception is a big desk, with a vase of flowers on top, and the lady behind it is wearing Western clothes and talking on the landline.

"One minute, please," she is telling me softly. She is even smiling at me.

Then, in a room with floors so shiny I am feeling that I will slip and fall on my behind, Sonali Khan herself is coming to take my hand.

"Lovely," she is saying, "I am so pleased you could come. Your video was touching me right here." And she is putting a palm to her heart. "I see audition videos all the time, but yours? It was something special.

"For you," she is explaining, "we are thinking about this role in my movie *What Do You Know About Mother's Love?* It will be about a single parent, a hijra, stigmatized by society, who is smashing—I mean *smashing*—all of society's rules by adopting a child on her own. A parent who is fierce, and ferocious, and full of love. A parent who lives life on her own terms. Blockbuster drama, mark my words. And we need a fresh face, authentic talent."

Her words are feeling to me like Azad's embrace when we were falling in love, like a tub full of syrupy roshogolla whose sugar is flowing in my veins, like Mr. Debnath accepting me to his acting class. It is feeling like Ragini's hands in mine, our laughter during the national activity of watching TV together in the evening.

"But listen," she is saying, putting her head close to mine, "one concern that my team has is, we want to avoid bad publicity. Your testimony for the terrorist—"

I am looking at the floor, showing shame. "Don't worry," I am saying. "She was my neighbor, but I am understanding now that maybe I was never really knowing who she was." The shame is burning in my cheeks.

"Good," Sonali Khan is saying. Then, in a normal voice, she continues, "Your video in which you were playing a mother, oof! Such feeling! Such emotion! Such drama in your eyes and voice! I said, 'This is a star being born right here. We must call her in.'"

After that, can you guess how my audition is going?

*

ON THE FIRST DAY of the shoot, in front of the studio doors, the whole unit is coming together, from driver to caterer to cameraman to director, and we are doing a prayer, then cracking a coconut for god's blessings. For all my life, everybody is believing that I am having a direct line to god, but I am knowing the truth. Whenever I am calling god, her line is busy. So today I am bowing my head deep. Please to let me act well today. Please to not let me get kicked off this film!

In my purse I am bringing my own lipstick, just in case, but after the prayer, when I am going into the makeup van, my eyes are growing big like pumpkins. This van is having a big mirror, lit up with rows of bright bulbs. On the counter, there are open boxes of pastes and powders and colors, wigs and little cotton sheets and glues and clips. Then the makeup artist, Hema, who is smiling and calling me madam, is using one of those soft cotton sheets to clean my face. I am smelling mint, like a chewing gum. The hair artist, Deepti, is pulling and tying, pinning this and gelling that. When I am saying, "Aaoo!" she is saying, "Oh, sorry, madam."

"Close your eyes, madam," Hema is gently saying, but how am I closing my eyes when they are making me look like a superstar in the mirror?

Inside the studio, which is a big warehouse with nothing stored inside it, I am walking carefully, looking at the ground for the cables that are running everywhere.

"Madam!" Someone is giving me a thumbs-up, a boy carrying silver umbrellas. "I saw your video!"

I am giving him a smile.

On the other end of the large studio is a set like the living room of my dreams—a big sofa, many plants, paintings on the walls, a cup of tea on a table. The cinematographer and director are making me sit here and sit there, stand at this angle or that angle. I am feeling afraid that my makeup will be melting.

Then the studio is becoming so quiet I am hearing somebody sniffle.

"Silence!" someone is calling.

"Rolling!" someone is calling.

"Action!" someone else is calling.

And me, from the depth of my heart, I am becoming the mother I am needing to be, even though the child actor will be coming tomorrow, and I am only imagining her today. Every wish of motherhood that I am having, for all my life, I am pouring into the lines they are giving me. I am dreaming this child into being before my eyes, and I am holding this beloved little person. How real is she, my child.

This child is having the face of Jivan, daughter of those poor parents, donor of pencils and textbooks. How is she living, alone in some dark cell? Even if she is not feeling the knife at her neck, I am feeling myself holding it. Now, my face thick with makeup, my hair stiff with gels, I am knowing what Arjuni Ma was truly telling me: In this world, only one of us can be truly free. Jivan, or me. Every day, I am making my choice, and I am making it today also.

"Daughter," I am telling this child, looking directly at the lens, "never let anyone tell you those lies. You are coming from the most precious place. Not from my womb, no, but from the deepest dreams of my heart."

"Cut it," the director is calling. When I am stepping behind the camera, looking at the small TV where my shot is playing, I am saying, "Excuse, excuse," to get through the dozen people crowding.

They are all wiping their eyes.

*

AT THE END OF THE DAY, when we are wrapping, Sonali Khan is personally coming to me. She is holding my arms and saying, "Lovely, you are going to be the country's next big star, you just wait!"

Then she is handing me an envelope and telling me to open it at home.

On the train, I am eating jhalmuri to celebrate, crunchy puffed rice and chopped cucumber in my mouth. I am walking past the guava seller and turning around. To him, for the first time, I am saying, "You give me three good ones!"

He is looking up and having a heart attack to see his new customer.

"Yes, it's me!" I am saying. "I am making a film now, so I am having to be fit! I am going to be eating fruits!"

In my room, I am eating a washed guava, and opening the envelope that Sonali Khan was giving me. Inside, there is a big glossy photo of me in scene.

I am finding some Sellotape and tearing it with my teeth. Then, beside my posters of Shah Rukh Khan and Priyanka Chopra, I am putting up this photo. Me, Lovely, in full hair and makeup, delivering a line to the camera in a Sonali Khan film.

The country is not knowing her yet, this new superstar. But me, I am knowing her.

PT SIR

ONE MORNING BEGINS WITH A RED SUN, LIGHT THAT slips around the curtain and finds his eyes, and it is the same as all other mornings, except it is wholly different. It is PT Sir's first day as an education secretary in the government.

PT Sir lingers for as long as he can bear it at home, then dashes to his new office. The city is wide awake. Flocks of schoolgirls, some holding hands, cross the street before his car. Their ironed and pleated skirts, their big laughs, tug at who he used to be. A boy scrubs dishes with ash in the gutter before a street-side booth hawking noodles. A stray dog trots along, no longer able to bother the man in his car.

Before the metal-detector gates of the state government building, turbaned guards salute PT Sir. He wonders whether they know who he is, or whether they salute anybody who arrives in a government-issue white Ambassador. One of the guards shows him to an elevator designated for use by VIPs only. In the rising compartment, heart drumming, PT Sir inspects his face in the shined metal doors. He may run into all sorts of VIPs in this building. From lobbyists to industrialists to movie stars, all have been known to discreetly visit this building.

On the seventh-floor corridor, PT Sir walks by a cleaning lady sitting on the pads of her feet, pushing a wet rag in wide arcs. She does not even glance up as he passes by.

PT Sir unlocks the door to his new office with a brand-new key. Inside, a tiny room, windowless. PT Sir closes the door behind him and sits in a chair with a high leather back. The chair tilts pleasingly under his weight. It rolls too, on wheels that don't get stuck. PT Sir sits like that for a few minutes, now and then tapping his fingers on the expanse of polished wood before him. Aside from a desktop computer and, puzzlingly, a packet of pencils, there is nothing else on the desk. The newness of it pleases him.

*

PT SIR KNOWS WHAT he has to do. He has to get his hands on Jivan's mercy petition, and add to it his recommendation, as a member of the new government, that the petition be denied. This is a criminal who deserves no mercy. The court's decision, the death penalty, ought to be carried out swiftly and with minimal burden to the taxpayer.

There is only one hitch: The mercy petition is with the girl's lawyer.

PT Sir picks up the phone and dials.

*

"SIR!" SAYS GOBIND INTO his phone, sitting up on one elbow in bed. His voice is thick with sleep. On the other end of the line is PT Sir, calling at an absurdly early hour. He asks after Gobind's wife, his parents, whether he has followed the cricket on TV lately.

"TV, sir," groans Gobind. "What are you saying, I have not sat down on my sofa for one minute. This case is taking everything, everything. You saw the disastrous ruling for my client."

And PT Sir begins his work.

"Bimala Pal was telling me," he begins smoothly, "well, you know what she was telling me? She was saying, 'That Gobind is a hardworking man.' She sees it. I see it. We all see your work. So I am just calling to convey that. You are a man of justice, and you are defending the girl, of course, that is your job."

Gobind says, "Kind of you to call about it, sir."

"But we all know," PT Sir continues, "what happened, I think."

Gobind is silent on the phone. Then he says, "Do we, sir?"

PT Sir laughs. He looks at his closed door, at the vents in the ceiling which gently pump cool air for his comfort. From somewhere, even he is not sure where, he has acquired a politician's persona. This big laugh was never his. "A man of principle," he says. "I like it.

"Gobind, listen," he continues, taking a deep breath, the laughter leaving his voice. "Justice in this case must be served. You think that. I think that. The public thinks that. So the long trial, the petitions, all of that I admire, believe me. But the court has shown this girl is guilty. Nobody"—his voice softens—"nobody feels more sad about that than me. She was my student. I saw her potential."

Gobind breathes noisily into the phone. He remains in his awkward position on the bed, afraid of the rustle of sheets, afraid of his footfall, afraid of missing any of what is being said.

"What I am saying is, it would be a shame if, after all this, the mercy petition hangs, going nowhere, for months and months. Don't you think so?"

PT Sir leans back in his chair. The chair, subservient, tilts. From Bimala Pal he has learned to withhold words in favor of long seconds of silence. They tick. He feels the man on the other end evaluating his words. Cautiously, Gobind says, "It's true, these petitions can take time."

"So," PT Sir declares, "why don't you hand the mercy petition to me. I will try to expedite it. Now I am in a position where I can expedite it, add my voice to it. We want swift justice, that is all I'm saying. Whatever outcome will be is not in my hands, but it is not good to keep the public waiting. It makes our new government look—"

He throws up a hand, a gesture of not knowing, though Gobind cannot see him.

"Let me send a messenger for it," PT Sir continues. "He will pick up the papers from you. And for your trouble, we will of course send you a small gift, just a token of thanks for your hard work on this case. You don't have to tell me, but I know how this work becomes a sacrifice—of family time, of time with children. Don't you have a daughter, Gobind? Doesn't she want more time with her papa, maybe a holiday next year?"

"Okay, sir," Gobind agrees. He is unsure if he chooses this.

JIVAN

UMA MADAM SAYS, "LOOK WHO HAS COME."

Who? I wipe sleep from my eyes and smooth the tangles of hair at the back of my head. A smell of cigarettes enters the room. The flash of gemstones up and down fingers. I stand. My skull, lifted so far from the ground, feels uncertain of itself.

My lawyer, Gobind, looks at me sorrowfully. Then he takes a deep breath which I can hear.

"What can I say? This case has become politicized. It is not even about you. I am sorry about the mercy petition. I truly did not think they would reject it."

"You told me they would let me go," I say. "Remember? You told me I am young, and I promised in my letter to be a teacher, serve anywhere in the country, dedicate myself to the country. I wrote all that in my letter. Then what happened?"

"Tell me," he says, after a pause, "are you getting enough to eat here? Do you want phone calls every day? I can try to bring you some magazines, something to read. What about a blanket? Is it cold here at night?"

"I . . ." I say after a while, my voice a croak. I have not had a drink of water all night, if this is morning. All day, if this is evening.

Then I find my voice.

"Am I cold?" I say.

"Enough food?" I spit.

"A magazine?" I scream.

"Stop it!" shouts Uma madam.

Gobind looks at my face, my bony body in the yellow salwar kameez, a reminder of sun. Soon the color will fade.

The lawyer looks at Uma madam, who is standing just outside the door, fiddling with the lock and key in her hand. She frowns at me.

"There is really nothing to do after the mercy petition is rejected," he says.

"Don't treat me like I am stupid," I shout. I don't know why I am shouting. I have a voice, I remind myself. This is my voice. It booms. It startles. "The country needs someone to punish," I tell him. "And I am that person."

"That blanket looks thin," Gobind says, his voice withdrawn. "What do you need to be comfortable? Better blanket, maybe."

"Blanket?" I say. "Blanket?"

I want to take off my slipper and whack him over the head with it. He is no better than a toilet cockroach.

"If you are not going to help me, then fine. I will write a hundred letters. I have time," I am shouting again. "I have time."

*

A COTERIE OF FLIES rises from a heap of—is that my shit? The sewage lines are blocked again. This late at night, someone walks up, sending the soft sound of bare feet on floor to my alert ears. "Uma madam!" I say. I am happy she has come. "It is you!"

But she does not respond.

Maybe it is only a rat.

Twice a day, a guard, a different guard, opens the gate and shoves in a plate of ruti and lentils, a watery soup specked with cumin or dirt, impossible to tell.

"Who is making ruti now?" I ask, but she doesn't answer. "It was my job. I was the one making ruti."

Roars of disgust rise from someone—me?—but in the end I eat, my back and my elbows working.

*

IT TAKES LONG FOR ME to get a notepad and a pen. The ink in the pen has dried, so I lick the nib to get the blue flowing.

In school, I learned how to write letters. I put the notepad on the ground, kneel before it in a posture of praying, and begin.

Dear Hon'ble Chief Minister Madam Bimala Pal,

This is in regards to my curative petition (BL9083-A). Respectfully I am writing to see if your office may please forward my petition one more time to the Council of Ministers in Delhi. As you know the evidence against me is circumstance-based. I am innocent. I lived in the Kolabagan slum, but I did not have anything to do with the train. If I am pardoned, I am willing to serve the nation for the rest of my life. My goal is to be a teacher, and teach English to the children living in poverty. Without me, my poor mother and father will have nothing left in their life. I am their only child.

Respectfully yours, your loyal citizen.

*

WAITING FOR SOME REPLY in the mail, I travel along with the letter in its hopeful van.

I travel along with the letter on a train, paddy fields outside.

I travel along with the letter in the air, on a plane where rich men eat chocolates.

But the letter lands on an indifferent desk.

Days pass. Weeks too. Maybe the minister's assistant glances at it, no more. Maybe they are overwhelmed by letters from prison.

Who am I except one of many?

My pen grows feeble.

What can words do? Not very much.

*

MY MOTHER DOESN'T COME this week. I wait alone, licking puffed rice from my palm, waiting for Uma madam to fetch me. I listen to the roar from the building above me grow and subside—a hundred conversations in one hour.

After the roar of the visitors is gone, I hear some repair work outside. It seems to me that a shovel scrapes on the other side of a wall. And then, a glorious thing. A hole, the size of a cigarette, opens up on a high wall. I see sun. In delight, I slam my palms on the wall.

But my palms make no sound. The wall, high above my head, is cold and feathery with algae. The scraping stops, eventually, and the repairmen go away, leaving me this present.

The light alerts me when morning comes. Now that I know it is morning, I practice the yoga I learned long ago, on rainy days in school. But my body is reluctant. It adheres, like a block of concrete, to the floor. There is nothing supple in my arms. They are twigs, waiting to snap. When I look down, my legs are dry and scaly, white with skin that is neither alive nor willing to shed.

*

IT IS EARLY WHEN Uma madam comes for me. She tells me to bathe.

"Has my mother come?" I say.

When I rise slowly on knees which creak, I wait for her to snap at me, but she doesn't. Softly she tells me to go to the bathroom, to use the toilet and take a bath.

Oh, a bath. I follow her to the bathroom, a spacious room whose walls and floor are brown with the filth of bodies, accumulated over the years. There stands a bucket of water, with a plastic mug floating in it.

Now Uma madam stands in the doorway, waiting for me to undress. She will stand there the whole time, her back turned to me if she is feeling kind.

"Do you have," I say, "any letters . . . ?"

Before she has said, "No! No letter! How many times do I have to tell you?"

Today she silently shakes her head.

I drop my clothes on the floor just outside the doorway, so they will not get wet. Inside, I crouch on the floor by the bucket. I can smell myself. I lift a mug of water and tip it over my head, and it drips over my oily hair, barely wetting it. The water is cold. Goose bumps rise on my skin. I feel a breeze that I did not know was there.

Another mug of water, and another.

I remember bathing as a child in the village, in the pond ringed by tal trees. My mother would press my head so I dipped in the green water, soap frothing about me. The bar of soap we used then was thin from her body. This bar is too. It is a sliver which I hold tight, or else it will fall and spin across the floor.

After I am dry and clothed, Uma madam waits for me to come out of the room, on my own. Nobody grabs me. The door is open. I step out. Then she locks the door, and there we are, standing in the corridor.

*

I COULD HAVE BEEN an ordinary person in the world. Ma, I could have gone to college, the city college where girls my age sit under trees, studying from their books, arguing, joking with boys. This is what I have seen in the movies.

Then I too would have given scraps of my meal to the stray dogs. I too would have had nostalgic corners of campus, corridor romances. I might have studied literature, and I might have spoken English so well that if you had met me on the street, Ma, you would not have known me! Ma, you would have thought I was a rich girl.

THE PAST TENSE
OF HANG IS HUNG

UNLESS WHAT IS BEING HUNG IS A PERSON, IN which case the word is "hanged." One morning, after the president of the country rejected her mercy petition, and before the journalists loitering outside the prison walls had a chance to crush their cigarettes underfoot and ask what was happening, Jivan was taken from her cell to the courtyard. As soon as she saw the platform, the length of rope thick enough to tether a boat to land, she fell. An attendant caught her. He was waiting for this purpose. In his arms, her body was a sack.

When she recovered, in the startling bright of the courtyard, she was given a minute to speak her last words. She licked her lips. Swallowed. Rubbed a cold palm on her kameez. "Where is my mother?" she asked. "Where is my father?"

She looked wildly about.

"You are making such a mistake," she said, voice cracking. "Minister madam, Bimala madam, see my letter. Please, have you got my letter?"

They were not there. Nobody was there, other than a few prison officials.

When Jivan was hanged, her neck snapped. The hair which had grown unruly during her time in prison fell over her face and drooped to her belly. The executioner, patches of sweat creeping up his armpits, shook his arms loose of the tension. A doctor, standing by with what looked like a receipt book, noted the time of death. Then a clerk went inside and dispatched a letter by speed post to inform Jivan's next of kin—a mother, in the Kolabagan slum—that her daughter had been killed by the state.

JIVAN

MOTHER, DO YOU GRIEVE?

Know that I will return to you. I will be a flutter in the leaves above where you sit, cooking ruti on the stove. I will be the stray cloud which shields you from days of sun. I will be the thunder that wakes you before rain floods the room.

When you walk to market, I will return to you as footprint on the soil. At night, when you close your eyes, I will appear as impress on the bed.

PT SIR

THE NEW APARTMENT COMES WITH LIGHTS BUILT INTO the ceilings. There is a balcony that an assistant has filled with potted plants. PT Sir accepts a window AC in the bedroom, though he declines ACs for the living room and the guest bedroom. He cannot hide the pleasure of no longer waking up sweating like a peasant.

He is now, he realizes, a cup of hot tea resting on the railing, a man who lives here, in a top-floor apartment in Ballygunge, a nice, upper-middle-class neighborhood of the city.

The party has seen fit to improve his salary. On top of that, it is true that very occasionally, educational institutions send him a little token in return for having their licenses and permits renewed in a timely manner.

Sometimes they go overboard. One private university offered him and his wife a week at a bungalow in Singapore, all expenses paid. He thought about it more than he would have liked to. Then he declined.

Nobody can say that PT Sir is not an ethical man.

*

IN THE FIELD CLOSE to the railway station, where PT Sir, then an ordinary teacher, first saw Katie Banerjee and Bimala Pal, a thousand men wait once more. They fill the field, its boundaries marked by lights which make day of the arriving dusk. Under the lights, unruly rows of ice-cream carts wander, no doubt announcing orange ices and cups of vanilla. PT Sir is too far away to hear. He is also too far to see the distant protesters, though he has been informed that they are there, university students who hold banners that say *Justice for Jivan.*

PT Sir stands high above the crowd, on the stage, before a microphone. He joins his hands and continues with his speech. "Soon after the people called for the terrorist to be brought to court," he says, "for the case to be swiftly resolved, look at how your ruling party handled it! Have you ever seen a government so attentive to the will of the people? Have you ever seen a government which demands that the courts move with speed?"

On he goes.

Among the frowning men in the crowd, some looking his way, others distracted by a pen of TV cameras off to the side, a woman stands, looking at PT Sir. She pays no attention to the man with the basket of chips who makes his way through the people. She pays no attention to a man with arms folded who digs his elbow in her side. When a breeze picks up, it fails to cause a ripple in her dupatta, the one she was not allowed to keep for modesty.

PT Sir knows who she is. Isn't she the ghost who begs him for mercy? Isn't she the ghost who searches the gaze of her teacher, hoping that he might offer rescue? Maybe that is why they had the white curtain up at the court—not so that Jivan could not influence his testimony, but so that he would not have to face her.

PT Sir's mouth speaks, while his eyes remain locked on hers.

"The vanquishing of good over evil is a signal! It is a signal of a party that listens to the public. It is a signal of a party that does what it promises!"

The crowd roars. They whistle and laugh. They wave flags raised high. One man is lifted onto another's shoulders, and a few TV cameras turn to capture this.

PT Sir surveys the crowd, his lips pulled into a smile, and when he looks for her once more, he cannot find her. The dust of the field tickles his throat, and PT Sir makes a fist before his mouth, takes a step back from the microphone, and coughs. From a bottle on the floor, he takes a sip of cold water. The irritation is gone.

When he speaks once more, his voice finds courage, and he finds courage too. Look at the rapt crowd. Look at the public, gathered before him, drinking in his words while he stands where Bimala Pal stood not so long ago.

By the end of the speech, he feels barely anchored

to the stage by his hands on the microphone, his whole self charged as if by the wind in the field and the electricity in the wires. When the crowd disperses, they fill buses where they hang from open doorways, and return to homes where the pride of the year is a new refrigerator. They will bend in fields, earning two rupees for crops that will sell in the city for forty, and stand by roadsides hawking stacks of dinnerware which will chip at first wash. They will watch, wide-eyed, the one movie that plays in the theater on their half day off from carpentry or construction or cleaning bathrooms, while PT Sir, in the government office's special elevator, moves upward.

ACKNOWLEDGMENTS

This book would not be in your hands without the tireless work and faith of Eric Simonoff and Jordan Pavlin. It has been a dream and an honor to have their creativity, their brilliance, and their generous hearts touch and transform this book. Immense gratitude also to magnificent Gabrielle Brooks, who took on this book and championed it in a way that has left me marveling.

My warmest thanks and admiration to the intimidatingly on-top-of-everything, smart people who have assisted them and given time and thought to this book: Jessica Spitz, Taylor Rondestvedt, Nicholas Thomson, and Demetris Papadimitropoulos.

I hope Sonny Mehta knew what it meant to me to receive his blessings. I treasure his memory.

I'm in awe of icons Ruth Liebmann, Paul Bogaards, Nicholas Latimer, and Emily Murphy for their advocacy, endless behind-the-scenes work, and for bringing such care to this book. A thousand thanks wouldn't be enough.

Gratitude to Kim Shannon for guiding me expertly and good-naturedly through my first galley signing.

Gratitude to Tyler Comrie for designing a gorgeous cover.

Acknowledgments

I know that a book comes into being because of the astute reads, creativity, and hard work of many, many people. My gratitude to the teams at WME, especially Fiona Baird, Laura Bonner, and Lauren Rogoff, and at Knopf, especially Ellen Feldman and Lara Phan. Thank you.

Warmest gratitude to my colleagues and mentors at Catapult, especially visionaries Andy Hunter, Pat Strachan, Jonathan Lee, and Nicole Chung, who have created a workplace full of trust and creativity, a workplace that cheers on writers, poets, and artists. Thank you for your extraordinary support.

Gratitude to guiding lights Katie Raissian, Mark Krotov, Alane Mason, James Meader, and Peter Joseph for including me in the literary community and lifting me—and many others—up.

Countless thanks to my teachers, especially Amy Hempel, Lynn Steger Strong, Colum McCann, Peter Carey, Nathan Englander, Veena Das, and Anand Pandian in the United States, and to all at Ashok Hall in Kolkata, especially Jharna Ganguli, Chaitali Sen, Mamta Chopra, and Sangeeta Banerjee.

My love and gratitude to Caroline Bleeke, for her incomparable kindness, wisdom, and steadfast friendship. Her faith has buoyed me through the years. Much of this book was written in the quiet of Caroline's living room. I will not forget it.

My love and gratitude to Laura Preston, whose groundbreaking writing inspires me to reach for greater complexity in my work. Our two-person workshops provided what I needed. It is in the light of Laura's generosity that this book has grown.

Immense gratitude to Julia Firestone and Jenny Shen for their early reads, insightful comments, and great enthusiasm. Many thanks to Mark Chiusano for offering encouragement and advice.

Love and gratitude to my friends Emma McGlennen, Alex Primiani, Sharon Wang, Maria Xia, Katie Vane, Mahum Shabir, Shreya Biswas, Rishika De, and Annesha Pramanik.

Love and gratitude to Beatrix Labikova, Ludovit Labik, Bea Labikova, Raphael Roter, and Halina Labikova. I got very lucky.

With this writing I seek to remember and hold close my beloved grandparents, who taught me to be curious, to be kind, and to revere books.

All my love to my mother and father, Sucharita and Partha Majumdar, who taught me to work hard, to live with discipline, and to dream. All my love to my sister, Roshni Majumdar, whose humor, drive, and ability to form communities wherever she goes I deeply admire.

All my love to Michal Labik, my husband, for his brilliant criticism of early drafts, for being a true partner in all things difficult and ordinary and joyous, and for his great friendship. Time with Michal is the best thing in the world. I am grateful.

A NOTE ABOUT THE AUTHOR

Megha Majumdar was born and raised in Kolkata, India. She moved to the United States to attend college at Harvard University, followed by graduate school in social anthropology at Johns Hopkins University. She works as an editor at Catapult and lives in New York City. *A Burning* is her first book. Follow her on Twitter @MeghaMaj and Instagram @megha.maj.

A NOTE ON THE TYPE

This book was set in Scala, a typeface created by the Dutch designer Martin Majoor (b. 1960) in 1988 and released by the FontFont foundry in 1990. While designed as a fully modern family of fonts containing both a serif and a sans serif alphabet, Scala retains many refinements normally associated with traditional fonts.

Typeset by Scribe, Philadelphia, Pennsylvania

Printed and bound by LSC/Harrisonburg,
Harrisonburg, Virginia

Designed by Betty Lew